★American

Like Sisters

Natalia Takes the Lead

★ American Girl®

Like Sisters

Natalia Takes the Lead

By Clare Hutton

Scholastic Inc.

Book design by Maeve Norton
Illustrations by Helen Huang

americangirl.com/service

ISBN 978-1-338-11502-4

10 9 8 7 6 5 4 3 2 1   18 19 20 21 22

Printed in the U.S.A.   23
First printing, 2018

For the best sister of all,
Lia Nigro

Chapter One

"Zoe! Think fast!" Natalia Martinez pitched a handful of fall leaves at her twin sister's head.

Zoe glared at her and shook her head so that the red and gold leaves fluttered to the ground. "Not funny," she said, picking a leaf out of her bangs.

Their cousin Emma, who was industriously raking on the other side of the lawn, laughed. "It's a little funny," she said.

Zoe made a face at them both, but her eyes were amused. "Messing up my beautiful hair," she complained with an exaggerated pout.

Zoe *did* have nice hair, Natalia thought.

Sometimes Natalia couldn't understand how she and Zoe could be identical twins. Right now, for instance, Zoe's preppy shirt and pants were as pressed and clean as if she'd just ironed them and put them on, even though she'd been wearing them all day. Her sleek dark bob swung neatly just below her chin, looking freshly combed.

Natalia, well . . . She glanced down at her own glittery but slightly rumpled sweater, which now had bits of leaf clinging to it, then smoothed a hand over her own long hair, which was frizzing out in all directions.

She *could* have looked as put-together as Zoe did, Natalia knew. If she wanted to get acquainted with the ironing board, and get her hair cut, and hang up her clothes as soon as they came out of the laundry, and sit and talk at recess instead of flinging herself across the playground to play tag—if she did all that, she and Zoe could look as identical as they were genetically.

But Natalia didn't care about that stuff. And Zoe did. And these differences, Natalia thought, were the real mystery.

"Twins are weird," she said out loud.

"Well, I didn't want to say anything," Emma joked, glancing up from her neat, small pile of leaves.

"I mean, look at us," Natalia said, gesturing back and forth between herself and Zoe. "For that matter, look at you. You're not a twin, but you're family. And you're the same age as us and we're in the same class at school. Why are we all so different?"

Natalia glanced around at Seaview House's wide front lawn, where they were raking. Even the lawn, Natalia thought, was like a tiny model of the differences between the three girls.

Generations of their family had lived in Seaview House, the oldest house in the small town of Waverly on the Chesapeake Bay. Just recently, Emma and her parents had moved in with Grandma Stephenson, who had gotten too old to want to live there by herself. Emma's mom was Natalia and Zoe's mom's twin sister, and they were turning the house into a bed-and-breakfast together. Emma and her parents were lucky enough to live at Seaview House. They had an apartment all to themselves on the top floor.

Natalia *loved* Seaview House, which was old in the best ways and full of cool things: a secret staircase concealed behind what looked like a regular wall, an attic crowded with stuff stored by more than a hundred years of ancestors, and a dumbwaiter, which was a tiny elevator for food. She was glad her mom and dad had bought a house just around the corner when they got married. But Seaview House had a *lot* of lawn. At their moms' request, the three girls had divided up the front lawn and had spent all Sunday morning raking it. Even divided into three, the lawn was huge, and a *lot* of work.

Emma had sectioned her part of the yard off into quarters. She worked intently on each quarter in turn, making small piles in their centers, a frown of careful concentration on her face, focused on getting up every last leaf. This was exactly what Emma was like, Natalia thought with a surge of affection: precise, and eager to do her best. Emma made lists and won swim meets and soccer games and worried about everything. She worked hard to do a good job at whatever she did.

Zoe, on the other hand . . . Natalia looked at her twin thoughtfully. What Zoe had actually gotten around to raking was almost as neat as what Emma had done. A couple mostly filled leaf bags leaned against a tree. Zoe liked to do things well, and she liked them to look *right*. But she hadn't done nearly as much as Emma, and Natalia knew it was because Zoe wasn't that interested in lawns. Right now, she wasn't raking at all, and she wasn't paying attention to what Natalia and Emma were saying, either.

Instead, she was looking at a bright red maple leaf, her head cocked thoughtfully to one side. As Natalia watched, Zoe crouched down—carefully not kneeling on the grass so that her pants stayed clean—and laid the leaf on the lawn between a smaller, almost pink one and a brilliantly golden gingko leaf.

"Oh no, we've lost her to the colors again," Natalia said to Emma. Zoe didn't even look up.

Zoe loved her family and her small group of close friends. She was snarky and funny and smart. But what she was most interested in was painting and drawing and making things. She could get swept up in examining a contrast of color or working on a sketch, and Natalia could see everything else melt away for her sister, leaving only the colors or the drawing.

Natalia herself didn't especially want to be able to

draw, but she couldn't help envying Zoe a little. Zoe knew what she was good at, knew what she was passionate about. Natalia did lots of stuff—theater and service club and volunteer work—but she didn't have one special interest or talent like Zoe did.

So, if Emma was careful and conscientious and Zoe was wrapped up in her art, what was she like? Natalia wondered. She looked at *her* part of the lawn. There was one big pile in the middle of her section of the lawn, bigger than any one of Emma's or Zoe's piles, but there were still tons of leaves threaded through the grass as well.

Natalia made a face. "Ugh, *why* do I have so many leaves left? I've been raking like crazy!" She had been putting all her energy into it, dragging huge rakefuls of leaves across the lawn. Why wasn't she as close to done as they were?

Zoe, distracted from her contemplation of colors, snorted.

"What?" Natalia asked, putting her hands on her hips.

"Well," Emma told her, exchanging a glance with

Zoe, "it's true that you've been working really hard. When you're working. But you keep getting—"

"Hello, girls!" Mrs. Lau from down the block was waving at them from the sidewalk, where she was pushing her baby in a stroller. Emma and Zoe both waved. Natalia hurried over.

"Hey, Mrs. Lau!" she said. "Were you guys down by the water?" She puffed her cheeks out at baby Charlie, making him giggle. "You like the beach, don't you, Charlie?" Charlie made babbling noises and reached up toward her, and Natalia took his plump little baby hands and smooched them.

She and Mrs. Lau chatted for a couple minutes. When Mrs. Lau and Charlie moved on, Natalia spotted old Mr. Ainsley, another neighbor, washing his car, and ran across the street for a minute to say hello.

When she came back, Emma raised her eyebrows pointedly.

"What?" Natalia asked.

"You were wondering why you haven't gotten a ton done?" Emma reminded her. "It's because Mr. Ainsley was probably the eighth person you've stopped to talk to since we started."

"I *like* to talk to people," Natalia said defensively. She reached down and picked up her rake. "Besides, I couldn't be rude and ignore them."

"You want to be friends with everybody," Zoe diagnosed. She reached down and pulled a lemon-colored leaf out of her pile and held it up, peering at it against the sun.

"Well . . . yeah," Natalia said, puzzled. Who *wouldn't* want to be friends with everybody? "Of course I do."

Emma leaned back against a tree and smiled at her. "And that's why we love you, Natalia," she said.

Seaview House's front door burst open as Natalia and Zoe's little brothers, six-year-old Tomás and five-year-old Mateo, ran outside, across the front porch, and down the steps to the lawn. Their elderly family dog, Riley, followed more slowly, puffing a little, and lay down by the front walk, his tail wagging.

Mateo and Tomás didn't stop. "Can't catch me!" Mateo screeched tauntingly, and sped across the lawn, running straight through Natalia's big pile and scattering two of Emma's smaller ones.

"Stop!" Zoe yelled, running to intercept the little boys as they headed for her part of the lawn. She was too late. Tomás tackled Mateo straight into the side of one of the bags full of leaves she'd raked and it toppled, spilling bright leaves between the trees. "No!" Zoe said, grabbing another bag to steady it before it fell, too. "Cut it out, you guys!"

"Keep them over there!" Emma called, hurriedly re-raking her own pile. "I'll come help you in a minute."

Natalia stuck two fingers in her mouth and whistled, a loud, shrill note. Mateo and Tomás untangled from each other and looked up at her, blinking.

"Come on!" she said cheerfully. "We'll play a game." The boys scrambled up and came over. She looked around her section of the lawn, a plan beginning to take shape. "Here," she said, handing her rake to Mateo. "We'll make a maze. And when we're done, Zoe and Emma will have to find their way through it."

Tomás nodded enthusiastically and started pushing

the leaves into walls, but Mateo leaned on the rake and frowned.

"We don't have enough leaves," he complained. "Emma and Zoe will be able to see over the walls."

"We could get leaves out of the bags," Tomás suggested.

"No, don't do that," Natalia said, seeing Emma's horrified face. "It would be cool to make really huge walls, but I'm not sure how we'd keep them up." She remembered a maze she'd seen once at a park. "What if instead of the kind with high walls, we just used low walls to mark out our maze?"

She crouched and picked up a stick to sketch a square in a nearby patch of dirt. "Pretend this is the maze. We could put the entrance here and the exit here." She drew little lines to show where she meant. "We can make it as complicated or as simple as we want—we just need to make sure there's only one way to get to the exit."

"We could make it look like a path by letting them get this far and then putting a wall," Tomás said, taking the stick and making scratches of his own. "They'll be so mad!" He giggled.

Once they'd marked out all the twists and turns, building the maze wasn't too hard. They all ran back and forth for a while, looking at their drawing before Natalia realized it would be easier to stand by the plan and direct Mateo and Tomás.

"Okay, Mateo," she said, squinting at the plan. "Put a long line of leaves up to where Tomás made the turn."

"What are you, the General of Leaves?" Zoe called teasingly from across the lawn.

"I'm the Commander of Autumn!" Natalia called back. "Obey me!" Emma and Zoe both rolled their eyes, but the boys, who loved playing army, saluted.

"Hut, hut, hut, double time," Natalia ordered. "Get those leaf walls built up, soldiers!"

There were long lines of red, yellow, and brown leaves crisscrossing Natalia's whole section of the lawn. "Almost ready," Tomás said, excited.

Zoe shook her head as she stuffed her last armload of leaves into a trash bag. "You know you're going to end up having to rake that whole side of the lawn again."

Natalia sighed. It was true. Still, at least the leaves

were all neatly laid out. Probably she and the boys could just scoop them up.

"Don't worry, we'll help you," Emma said supportively.

Zoe grinned. "I suppose. But only if the maze is fun."

The maze *was* fun.

"This is actually impossible, isn't it?" Emma asked, a line of concentration appearing between her eyebrows.

"You're never going to get it!" Mateo teased, jumping up and down, and Zoe and Emma both groaned.

Tomás, looking sympathetic, whispered loudly, "Emma! Turn here!"

Natalia flopped down cross-legged on the lawn to watch Zoe and Emma puzzle their way through. Riley, wagging his tail, walked over stiff-leggedly and collapsed next to her, putting his head in Natalia's lap.

"Hey there, good boy," Natalia said, playing with Riley's long, silky ears. "Whatcha doing? You want to play?" Riley woofed softly and closed his eyes.

"You all look busy." Her mother's amused voice came from above her, and Natalia twisted around to look up at her.

"Hey!" Natalia said. "I didn't hear you come out." Then she remembered what she was supposed to be doing and grimaced. "Sorry, we *were* raking, I swear."

"I know," her mom said, smiling. "But come on inside, because Aunt Amy and I have news for you." She raised her voice. "Emma! Zoe! You, too."

Emma was just triumphantly stepping out of the maze. "What?" she said. "We're going to clean it up! It's not Natalia's fault!"

"Well, it actually is," Zoe muttered, still stuck halfway through the maze. At Emma's look, she sighed and added, "But we are going to help clean up."

"You're not in trouble," Natalia's mom said. "Just come inside. We have something exciting to tell you."

In the elegant front room of Seaview House, Emma's mom, Aunt Amy, was waiting. Natalia and Zoe's mom sat down next to her on the long velvet settee and waved the girls into cushy armchairs.

As Natalia looked at her mom and aunt, she was reminded again of how different she and Zoe were, because their mom and Aunt Amy, who were twins, too, were just as unlike each other. Aunt Amy, who had been a lawyer in Seattle before coming back to Waverly, looked very businesslike. She had short, neat hair and wore blazers and nice pants and shoes with a low heel on them. Natalia's own mom was more a classic-mom type: shoulder-length hair, sweaters, and sneakers. But they shared the dream of turning Seaview House into a bed-and-breakfast, and they worked together really well.

"So what's up?" Zoe asked curiously.

Natalia's mom and Aunt Amy looked at each other. "Well . . ." Aunt Amy said, drawing out the anticipation, ". . . we have our first guests!"

"What?" Natalia said. "That's amazing!" Zoe and Emma cheered. Her mom and Aunt Amy had been working on fixing Seaview House up for months and, except for a reception for friends and family, they hadn't opened for business yet. Apparently, getting ready for guests took a *long* time.

"We have two couples coming for three full weeks. They're friends and they're traveling together," Natalia's mom said. "They sounded lovely on the phone."

"We could work to make their stay better. I can help Dad in the kitchen," Emma offered. "I like cooking."

"Do you want me and Zoe to wait tables?" Natalia asked. "That could be fun."

Zoe frowned, twisting a strand of hair around her finger. "Do I have to? I'd rather make beds or something like that. I don't want to have to talk to strangers first thing in the morning. Ugh."

Their mom laughed. "Don't worry, Zoe, I think we can handle four guests. We can come back to the idea when the bed-and-breakfast starts getting busier. But if we ever do need you girls to help out, it'll be your choice. And I imagine you'd get paid."

"Well, congratulations," Emma said. "The guests are going to have a great time."

"I hope so." Aunt Amy sighed. "Each couple is bringing a dog with them. They asked if I could recommend a dog-walking service or doggy day care around here, but I couldn't. They decided to come anyway, but it means they'll have to schedule their days around walking the dogs."

Zoe and Natalia's mom shook her head. "I really wish

we could have found another option for them. Those dogs are going to get restless."

A brilliant idea hit Natalia, and she bounced in her seat. "What if *we* walk the dogs? I love dogs!"

Her mom and Aunt Amy exchanged a look. "Are you sure?" Aunt Amy asked. "You'll be responsible for taking them out twice every day. If you're going to do it, you'll have to make a commitment and stick to it."

"Of course we'll stick to it," Natalia said.

"I want to help," Emma said hesitantly. "But I've got soccer practice twice a week and games as well. And swim team practice, too."

"And I'm going to do theater club with Natalia this year," Zoe said, not making eye contact with anyone.

"You *are?*" Natalia asked, distracted. Zoe had never wanted to sign up for theater club before. "Are you going to paint sets?"

Zoe's cheeks were turning pink. "I might try out for Dorothy," she mumbled. "I really like *The Wizard of Oz.*"

Of course. Natalia knew that was her sister's favorite musical. "I think that's great," she said decidedly. "You've got a way better singing voice than I do."

Zoe peeked at her from the corner of her eye. "Do I?"

"You really do," Natalia assured her.

"It sounds like you girls are pretty busy," Natalia's mom said, biting her lip. "It's a good idea, though. Maybe there's someone at your school who would like—"

"No!" Natalia said. "We want to do it. Come on, you guys. There are three of us, and only two dogs, for just a few weeks. It'll be easy."

"Well . . ." said Emma.

"I guess . . ." said Zoe.

"Awesome," Natalia said confidently. Between the three of them, they'd have plenty of time. "We'll do it," she said to her mom and Aunt Amy. "Trust me, it'll be a piece of cake."

Chapter Two

"It's going to be so fun," Natalia told her best friend, Caitlin, the next day at school. "You should help, too. You like dogs. And we'll get paid."

"It does sound fun," Caitlin said, setting out two pencils, an eraser, and a pencil sharpener in a straight line above the edge of her notebook. "But I don't have time. Sorry."

Natalia sighed. Why was everyone so worried about having time for this? You *made* time for the things that you wanted to do. "What're you doing that's taking so much time?" she asked. "You're not that busy." Caitlin was on student council with her, but she couldn't think of anything else that would keep her from walking dogs a couple days a week.

"I have a master plan," Caitlin said. She looked serious, but there was a suppressed laugh in her voice.

"As usual," Natalia said. She was pretty sure Caitlin was going to end up president, or maybe a super-villain. She was a very organized girl. "What is it this time?"

"I'm going to get straight A's this semester," Caitlin said. "I'm tired of your cousin outclassing me." She shot a quick glance over her shoulder to where Emma was getting out her own notebook.

"You need to get over this competitive thing you have with Emma," Natalia advised. Caitlin and Emma weren't fighting anymore, the way they had at the very beginning of the school year, but Caitlin was still kind of weird about Emma.

"It's not really Emma. I *like* Emma," Caitlin said seriously. "I just don't like people being better than me, and Emma's the best student in the class."

Natalia didn't see the point in pursuing *that* any further. As long as Emma and Caitlin were nice to each other, she guessed Caitlin could use Emma to motivate herself to study. "Still," she argued, "that's not going to take *all* your time."

"And I want to be Glinda the Good Witch in *The Wizard of Oz*," Caitlin told her. "This is our last year in the kids' theater program. Next year, we'll be in the teen group, and we'll be the youngest ones and won't get good parts for ages. This is my chance. But I have to rehearse and rehearse to be perfect."

Natalia frowned. "I'm trying out for the Wicked Witch of the West, but I'm not going to give up everything else."

Caitlin raised an eyebrow. "If you're serious about it, maybe you should."

"I *am* serious about it," Natalia insisted. "I've been practicing my cackle since they announced it was the play this year. I'm going to get long fake fingernails so I can menace Dorothy better." She wiggled her fingers at Caitlin threateningly. "But I can do other things, too."

Caitlin shrugged. "Okay, if you're sure."

Ms. Patel, their math teacher, cleared her throat at the front of the room, and Caitlin picked up a pencil, opened her notebook, and waited attentively.

Natalia shook her head. She wanted to be in the play, too, and to get good grades, but sometimes Caitlin was just too intense.

Ms. Patel began to write on the board, and Natalia rolled her pencil between her fingers. What kind of dogs would the B and B guests have? she wondered. A beagle would be nice—they had such cute little faces. She drew a floppy-eared puppy in the margin of her notebook. Or a husky would be sweet, too. They were such pretty dogs.

There was a dog in *The Wizard of Oz*. What if one of the dogs that came to the B and B turned out to be the perfect Toto? She pictured a tiny black terrier, like Toto in the movie, following patiently at Zoe-as-Dorothy's heels. Natalia could swoop it up in her arms, cackling, "And your little dog, too!"

Of course, Natalia reminded herself, the guests with the dogs would be gone long before the play was performed. If the dog was absolutely perfect, though, maybe they would want to stay so they could see him onstage. Or they would leave him with Natalia until the play.

"Natalia!" Ms. Patel's voice cut through her daydream. At the same time, Caitlin nudged her in the ribs with a sharp elbow. Natalia jerked to attention.

"Yes, Ms. Patel?" she asked politely.

The teacher frowned. "Please pay attention, Natalia. For the second time, can you tell me what y would be in the problem on the whiteboard?"

Natalia looked at the board. The problem read $6 = 2\,(y + 2)$

She had to multiply the equation by 2, she knew that. Or was she supposed to add 2?

"Is y four?" she guessed. "And if not, y not?" Natalia grinned brightly at her own joke, and some of the other kids giggled.

Ms. Patel pursed her lips, unamused. "We have a midterm coming up, Natalia, and it's going to cover everything you've learned so far this year. If you're planning to do well, you need to *pay attention in class.*" She looked at Caitlin. "Caitlin, can you give us the answer and explain how you got it?"

"One," Caitlin said instantly. "First you divide six by two to figure out that the equation in the parentheses should equal three and then—" She went on talking, but Natalia tuned out, thinking of puppies and of the fun of being the Wicked Witch of the West. *Green face paint,* she thought dreamily. *And lots of black shadow around my eyes so I look really evil. Zoe'll help me with that.*

She was half listening, and when Ms. Patel said, "Do you understand now, Natalia?" she snapped to attention.

"Absolutely!"

༄

After school, Zoe had art club and Emma had soccer practice, so Natalia headed over to Seaview House to see what the grown-ups were up to. Her mom, Aunt Amy, and Grandma Stephenson were sitting at the table in the kitchen, a bunch of dried flowers spread out in front of them and a pile of books to the side.

"What are you doing?" Natalia asked, dropping her backpack just inside the door. The kitchen was full of warm smells—something sweet and cinnamony—and the counters and range were shining, meticulously clean.

"Now that the summer flowers are dying, there's not much left in the gardens except chrysanthemums," her mother told her. Seaview House had beautiful gardens, going down in terraced levels toward the bay. All summer different flowers blossomed, filling the air with their scent, and Natalia's mom and Aunt Amy had cut armloads to decorate Seaview House.

"Your grandmother's been drying flowers all summer," Aunt Amy said. "We were going to make up bouquets to put in the bedrooms."

Natalia looked at the piles of dried flowers on the table. There were a few she recognized: roses, lavender, baby's breath. But while most of them looked vaguely familiar, she couldn't identify the rest by name.

"And we thought it would be interesting to figure out the meaning of each flower and say something with the bouquets," Grandma Stephenson said briskly. "We have a lot of these flower books, and the guests could look up the meanings of their bouquets. Maybe we can give them a prize if they figure out the secret message."

That definitely sounded like a Grandma Stephenson idea, Natalia thought. She had two grandmothers: Abuelita, who lived with Natalia's family a few blocks away, and Grandma Stephenson, who lived with Emma's family here in Seaview House.

Abuelita was cozy and solid. She had been a nurse, and she was good at taking care of people. She made you feel like you were precious and special just for being yourself. Grandma Stephenson had been a teacher. She liked to see people learn and wanted them to investigate things and figure them out. She made you feel like you were working for her approval, and when she gave it, you felt like you had achieved something.

"Okay." Natalia joined them at the table. "Can I help?"

"We'll put flowers together, and you look and tell us what they mean," her mother suggested.

Aunt Amy passed her a doughnut from the counter. "Cinnamon apple," she said. "Brian made them this morning."

That explained the tantalizing smells. Uncle Brian, Emma's dad, had been a chef before he came to Waverly, and he was going to cook all the food for the bed-and-breakfast—once the first guests arrived, that is.

Natalia bit into the doughnut and closed her eyes in

bliss. It was delicious, with a crispness to the outside and a light chewy interior. *Really* good.

"What are these?" her mom asked, and Natalia opened her eyes to see her mom holding a white flower with widespread petals.

"Star of Bethlehem," Grandma Stephenson told them. "It's a kind of lily."

Natalia picked up one of the books and searched through it. "It says it means 'hope.'"

"Seems reasonable." Her mom picked up some lavender and laid it next to the lily. "What about this?"

Lavender, apparently, meant "distrust."

"I'm not sure that's a good message," Natalia said. "Hope and distrust? Like you don't trust the guests, but you hope you're wrong about them?"

The phone rang and Aunt Amy got up to answer it.

"Hmm." As Aunt Amy began to talk to the caller, Natalia's mom shuffled through the flowers. "How about the roses?" she asked. "Everyone loves roses."

"I'm so sorry to hear that," Aunt Amy said into the phone, and everyone turned to look at her, concerned.

She waved a hand in the air in a "don't worry about it" gesture.

"Roses mean different things depending on what color they are," Natalia said. "Red ones mean 'passionate love.'"

"Hope and passionate love seem like an odd message to get from your innkeeper," Grandma Stephenson pointed out.

"I think we could do that, if you have so much already organized," Aunt Amy said. Her phone voice was cheerful and professional, but there was a small worried frown on her face.

"A *lot* of these flowers have weird meanings coming from someone you don't really know," Natalia said, running her eyes over the pages of her book. "Like a rhododendron means 'beware,' and heather means 'solitude.'"

"I'm not sure *what* we want to say to the guests," Grandma Stephenson said, "but it does seem like we're going to have to limit what flowers we use if we want their meaning to be reasonable."

Natalia closed the book and picked up a few Stars of

Bethlehem and some lavender, along with some leaves and baby's breath. They looked nice together. "I don't think this idea is working out," she told her mother and grandmother. "I think we should just put together something pretty and not worry about what it means."

Grandma Stephenson laughed and looked at her approvingly. "You're absolutely right," she said. "Sometimes I get so caught up in my ideas that I don't realize they're not very practical. Thank you for setting me straight, Natalia."

"I see," Aunt Amy said into the phone. "We might actually have a solution to that. Can you hold on for a moment?"

She muted the phone. Her eyes were shining with excitement.

"You know that the Liberty Inn over in Middleton had a fire?" she asked breathlessly. Middleton was about ten miles away.

"It did?" Natalia asked, surprised. She had eaten dinner at the Liberty Inn a couple times. It was bigger than Seaview House, more a proper inn than a bed-and-breakfast.

"Yes," her mom said. "They didn't have much damage, though. What about it, Amy?"

"Well," Aunt Amy said, drawing the word out a little, "the only real damage was to their dining room and the patio outside. But the couple I have on the phone right now was planning to get married there in three weeks, on the patio, and to have their reception in the dining room. They don't want to postpone the wedding, so they're looking for a new venue."

Natalia's mom gasped, her eyes widening. "A *wedding*? In three weeks? It would be wonderful, but I don't think we could."

"It's only a small wedding," Aunt Amy said. "Minuscule. Thirty people. And they want it simple. They've made arrangements with a florist and for a cake and so on already, so it would just be the food and the venue."

Natalia's mom gave a tiny smile. "It would have to be, to put it on in just a few weeks. But maybe . . ."

"I think it's a wonderful idea," Grandma Stephenson said firmly. "You girls have been dreaming about this kind of thing for years. It'll be a real rush and a lot of work, but you could start making your reputation in a hurry."

Natalia thought it sounded wonderful. Weddings were *fun*—everyone happy and in love—and she couldn't think of a better place to celebrate than Seaview House.

"There's one other thing," Aunt Amy said, looking at Natalia. "The couple is planning to use their dogs as ring bearers."

Natalia's heart began pounding faster.

Grandma Stephenson raised her eyebrows. "My goodness," she said wryly.

"Well, their dogs are important to them, Mother," Aunt Amy said. "They'd be bringing the dogs down with them, and they'd need help walking them while they're making the arrangements, and then to have someone look after the dogs on the big day."

"Four dogs seem like a lot," said Natalia's mom.

But Natalia shook her head. A wedding at Seaview House? How cool would that be?! Surely her mom and aunt weren't going to throw away an opportunity like this because they thought looking after four dogs would be too much for Natalia, Zoe, and Emma!

"It's no problem," she said quickly. "It sounds like fun. And I know Emma and Zoe would love to help, too. It'll be easy with all three of us."

Briefly, it crossed her mind that Zoe and Emma had been worried about spending a lot of time looking after *two* dogs. But they were worriers. And this was a wonderful opportunity!

And after all, how much trouble could just four dogs be?

Chapter Three

"If you decide to audition for a role in *The Wizard of Oz*, you must be prepared to commit," Ms. Andrews, the theater club director, said. "It's a big, exciting musical, and a show that everyone knows and loves. Because everyone loves it so much, as actors, we have a *responsibility* to do our absolute best to know our parts and give the best performances we're capable of."

Natalia snuck a glance at her watch. It was four o'clock. The two couples with the dogs were supposed to be checking in to Seaview House just about now. She and Emma and Zoe were going to go over and meet the dogs after the theater club meeting.

Suppressing a sigh, she glanced at Zoe on one side of her, then at Caitlin on the other. Both of them were leaning forward intently, their eyes fixed on Ms. Andrews.

Natalia shifted in her seat and tried to refocus and pay attention, too. It wasn't that Natalia didn't care about the play; she did. And she liked Ms. Andrews and she was excited to be in *The Wizard of Oz*. It was just that she couldn't wait to meet the dogs. At least for today, the end of the theater club meeting couldn't come fast enough.

Partly, it was because this was Natalia's third year in the theater club. Her first year, they'd done *Oliver!* and Natalia had been an orphan. Last year, they'd done *Annie*, and Natalia had been a different orphan.

Which had been great. Natalia really loved being onstage, even if she was just jumping around and singing in chorus with a bunch of other kids. But this was going to be Natalia's year. She wasn't a great singer, and usually, in musicals, you had to be able to sing to get a good part. But the Wicked Witch of the West was an amazing part: big and loud and exciting. And you didn't have to be able to sing. The Witch didn't sing at all—she cackled and shouted and commanded flying monkeys, but she didn't have to carry a tune.

So, Natalia was excited about the show, in general.

But she'd heard Ms. Andrews give more or less the same speech both years. Next, they would do some stretches and some voice exercises, and then Ms. Andrews would hand out scripts for the auditions next week. Except for getting the scripts, it was kind of a waste of time.

Natalia wondered what kinds of dogs would be waiting at Seaview House. She still thought it would be wonderful if one of them would make a good Toto. But, besides the fact that they wouldn't be staying that long, a Toto would have to be awfully well behaved, because he'd be onstage basically the whole time.

Now that she thought about it, she was pretty sure Ms. Andrews might just want to have whoever played Dorothy carry around a stuffed dog in a basket.

"Natalia!" Zoe whispered.

With a start, Natalia realized that Ms. Andrews had wrapped up her speech about their responsibility toward the audience and that everyone was on their feet and crowding up toward the stage. Everyone except Natalia.

It must be time to stretch. Natalia hopped to her feet and hurried after the others. Her cheeks were hot with embarrassment. Ms. Andrews didn't say anything, but she eyed Natalia disapprovingly, as if she was quite aware that Natalia had been daydreaming, and she didn't think much of an actress who couldn't pay attention to her director.

"Okay," she said, once all the kids were in a circle on the stage. "We're going to start by loosening up. Let's reach toward the sky."

With the others, Natalia stretched and reached, and, as Ms. Andrews instructed, then she slowly, *slowly* bent over, trying to move one vertebra at a time, and let her body hang relaxed, her fingers brushing the floor.

"Breathe in deeply," Ms. Andrews said. "Then, slowly, let your breath out in a steady stream as you roll back up."

They rotated their shoulders and their necks, shook out their hands, and made faces, stretching their eyes and mouths wide, then scrunching their faces tightly. Natalia looked to see what her sister was making of all this. Zoe was usually wary of anything that might make her look silly. But Zoe was smiling, bouncing a little on the balls of her feet as she shook and stretched. She caught sight of Natalia looking at her and wiggled her eyebrows. She was having fun.

After about ten minutes of stretches and of yowling deep in their chests and then high in their throats, stretching their voices like they did their bodies, Ms. Andrews finally made the announcement Natalia had been waiting for.

"Okay, kids," she said cheerfully. "Good work! I'm going to pass out audition scripts for the various roles. Raise your hand when I call the part you're interested in. It's okay to audition for more than one role, but I expect you all to be word perfect in the audition scenes for tryouts next Monday. If you're not interested in a major role, speak to me at the end of club, and we'll sign you up for the chorus. Let's start with Dorothy."

Flushing slightly, Zoe raised her hand, along with eleven other girls. Her eyes were bright, and her lips were pressed tightly together. Natalia stared at her in surprise. It was so *weird* to see Zoe nervous about something.

Ms. Andrews called the Scarecrow, the Tin Man, and the Cowardly Lion next. For a minute, Natalia wondered if maybe she should try out for the Scarecrow, too. She pictured herself and Zoe, side by side, onstage together for almost the whole musical. It would be really fun. And the Scarecrow had a floppy, falling-over dance that Natalia knew she'd enjoy.

But the Scarecrow also had to sing a lot. As five or six other kids raised their hands, Natalia kept hers down.

When Ms. Andrews called for prospective Glinda the Good Witches, Caitlin and several other girls raised their hands. Taking her script, Caitlin looked around at the other girls thoughtfully, weighing up her competition.

"Any Wicked Witches of the West here?" Ms. Andrews asked, and Natalia's hand shot up into the air. There were six other hands up, she saw. Two of the girls she didn't know; they were new to theater club this year. One of the other girls, Charlotte, had been in the chorus with Natalia for both *Oliver!* and *Annie*. She was nice, and she sang better than Natalia did, when you could hear her. But she was always super-quiet onstage, too shy to speak out. She probably wasn't going to be much competition.

The other three were good actresses, Natalia thought. There was one girl, Darcy, who was the tallest girl in the club, and who had a big voice that projected easily from the stage. *She's probably my main competition,* Natalia thought. *And she's good. But I'm going to be better.*

⁓

When Natalia and Zoe got to the inn, Emma was sitting on the steps outside waiting for them. She was still in her soccer uniform, looking sweaty and tired.

"Why are you out here?" Zoe asked. Emma lived in Seaview House, so she didn't need to wait to be asked in.

"I feel weird going in with guests there," Emma whispered. "I thought I'd wait for you guys."

"You're going to have to get used to it or you're going to have a tough time living in a bed-and-breakfast," Natalia said practically. Then she looked at the door. Suddenly, it did feel a bit weird to walk in if there were strangers there. Paying strangers, who were living in Seaview House for their vacation. "We'll all go in together," she said in a hushed voice.

Emma pushed open the front door cautiously, Zoe and Natalia right behind her.

The front parlor looked warm and lovely, glowing lamps lighting up the deep red of the walls and the golds and blues of the furniture. By the piano, two strange couples stood laughing with Natalia's mom and Aunt Amy. They all had glasses of wine, and there was a plate of Uncle Brian's hors d'ocuvres on top of the piano.

The people looked nice enough. But where were the dogs?

"Girls!" Aunt Amy turned to greet them with a smile. "Come and meet Mr. and Mrs. Goldstein and Mr. and Mrs. Warner."

Natalia and her sister and cousin came over and awkwardly shook hands. Mr. Goldstein asked Emma about her soccer team, and Mrs. Warner asked the twins what grade they were in and how they liked school and all the questions adults normally asked kids they didn't know.

Natalia and Zoe answered politely, but the whole time, Natalia was looking around the parlor for any sign that two dogs were in residence at Seaview House. But there was nothing: no collars, no food bowls, no chew toys.

Zoe was telling Mrs. Warner that she liked social studies when Natalia broke in. "Did you bring the dogs?" she asked eagerly. It would be terrible if, after all the discussion, they had left the dogs somewhere else instead.

All the adults laughed. "I told you they couldn't wait," Natalia's mother said.

"They're on the back porch," Mrs. Goldstein said. "We thought you girls could take them for a little walk and get to know each other."

"Sounds great," Natalia said cheerfully. Zoe shrugged and nodded. Emma looked more tired than ever, but she gave a polite smile.

"If you take the job, we thought we'd pay you twenty dollars a day for the walks," Mr. Warner added. "Does that sound like enough?"

The girls exchanged wide-eyed glances. *Twenty dollars a day for twenty-one days would be over four hundred dollars*, Natalia realized. For playing with dogs! "That sounds great," she said quickly, and Emma and Zoe nodded.

The dogs were lounging on the screened back porch, but they hopped up when the back door opened. A big black dog waved his tail politely, but a tiny tan terrier yapped hysterically, jumping up at them.

"Good girl, Daisy," Mrs. Goldstein said, patting the terrier. "She's just excited to see you."

Natalia knelt down and petted Daisy's head. The little dog writhed around ecstatically, craning her head to lick Natalia's hand.

"And this is Jasper," Mr. Warner said. Emma rumpled Jasper's ears and smiled when the black dog began to pant happily.

Zoe and Natalia fastened leashes to the dogs' collars and all three girls took the two dogs out into the neighborhood. Jasper walked close beside Zoe, his tail wagging steadily. Daisy bounced along the pavement, stopping to sniff at everything they passed—trees, rocks, lampposts, the tires of cars parked along the street—and then hurrying ahead to the next object on her route. There was a squirrel busily sniffing along the yard of the house next door and Daisy yapped excitedly, straining at the leash.

"It's a good thing she's so little," Natalia said, holding her back. "It's okay, Daisy, look, you've scared it off. It *respects* you." Once the squirrel had disappeared up a tree, Daisy gave up and strutted on.

"They are pretty cute," Zoe said.

Emma agreed. "They're both nice dogs. It'll be fun to walk them. And I guess two dogs between the three of us won't take that much time."

"Um," said Natalia, then stopped. She hadn't yet told Emma and Zoe about the wedding at Seaview House, or that she'd promised they'd look after two more dogs. But maybe now wasn't the right moment.

Zoe stopped dead. Jasper tugged at the leash, and then turned back to look at her curiously.

Emma looked back and forth between Zoe and Natalia. "What's going on?" she asked.

"I know that look on your face, Natalia," Zoe said ominously. "There's something you aren't telling us, isn't there?"

Natalia bit her lip nervously. "Well, some people called Seaview House a few days ago while I was there and asked if they could have a wedding there. In three weeks. The place they were going to do it had a fire."

"A wedding?" Emma said curiously. "That's a big deal! Is my dad making all the food?"

Zoe's steady gaze stayed fixed on Natalia's face. "That's not all, though, is it?" she asked. "You look *guilty*."

"I'm not *guilty*," Natalia said, mimicking her twin's voice. "It's going to be a lot of fun. You guys will thank me."

Now Emma was looking decidedly nervous. "What do you mean, that's not all?" she asked. "And why will we thank you?"

"They have two dogs that are going to be ring bearers," Natalia explained. "And I told Mom and Aunt Amy that we'd be happy to take care of them, too. They need us to walk them during the days leading up to the wedding when they're here making arrangements, and then on the day of the wedding."

"Natalia!" Zoe scolded. "You don't have the right to make promises for us without asking."

"But a wedding will be so great!" Natalia insisted. "They were on the phone asking, and Mom and Aunt

Amy needed an answer about the dogs so they could say yes or no to the wedding. You wouldn't want them to turn down a wedding at Seaview House, would you?" Daisy tugged on the leash, and Natalia started walking again. Emma and Zoe hurried after her.

"Having a wedding here will be awesome, but I have soccer and swim practice during the week," Emma said apologetically. "I wish you had asked me first."

"I'll do most of it, I swear," Natalia promised. "You guys won't have to do anything except show up and play with the dogs when you have free time. It'll be fun. And think about the money. They'll be paying us, too!"

"What about school?" Zoe said dubiously. "We have midterms coming up. And what about the play? There are going to be rehearsals starting once Ms. Andrews chooses the cast."

"It'll be fine," Natalia assured her. She looked down at happy, wiggly Daisy and dignified Jasper. They were great, and walking them was a piece of cake. "These dogs are no trouble at all," she told the others. "You don't have to worry, because I've got this."

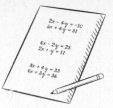

Chapter Four

As she walked up the school steps the next morning with Caitlin, Natalia's phone buzzed in her backpack.

"Go ahead," she told Caitlin. "I'll catch up in a minute." Zoe had already disappeared into school with her friends Louise and Ava.

Stepping to the side, Natalia dug out her phone and read her new text. It was from her mom.

The bride and groom are coming this afternoon! The text was followed by emojis of champagne glasses. Natalia chuckled and rolled her eyes. Her mom was such a dork sometimes.

The phone beeped again. *They're bringing the dogs, so come over after school! They want to meet you. Tell Zoe and Emma.* Several dog-face emojis followed.

Grinning, Natalia texted back, *We'll be there!* then turned off the phone. They were allowed to take their phones into school, but they weren't allowed to have them on once classes started.

I can't wait, Natalia thought as she sat down in math class. Yesterday afternoon had been a total success. They'd taken the dogs for a long walk, and then thrown balls for them on the long lawn of Seaview House. Jasper had been amazing, leaping in the air to catch any ball that went near him. Daisy, with her shorter legs, had trundled busily behind him each time they threw the ball, returning panting happily without the ball after Jasper caught it.

Emma, who liked things to be fair, had thrown the ball directly to Daisy several times, but she had just dropped it immediately, cocking her head expectantly at them. She didn't seem to know what to do with it. Then Jasper had stolen it from her, and she had been happy again.

It had been a lot of fun. And today would be even better—two more dogs for the three of them to play with!

Or maybe even the four of them . . . four dogs and four girls would be perfect.

"They were *so* cute," she told Caitlin, who was lining up her school supplies as usual. "I bet the new dogs will have a ton of fun with them. I wish you'd change your mind and help us with the dog walking. Emma and Zoe are both so busy, they won't mind splitting the money four ways."

"*I'm* just as busy as they are," Caitlin said. "And you should be, too. This dog stuff is going to take up more time than you think it is."

Caitlin is being so negative, Natalia thought, flipping her hair behind her shoulder. *If she worries about everything, she's going to miss out on a lot.*

"Settle down, everyone," Ms. Patel said at the front of the classroom. "Get out your homework from last night and we'll go over it."

Natalia froze, her heart sinking. She had *completely* forgotten her math homework. She'd scribbled the answers to a social studies worksheet before the theater club meeting, but she hadn't had a chance to do her math, too. Then, by the time they'd finished with the dogs, she'd totally forgotten. Forgotten until now.

Natalia pulled out her folder and pretended to shuffle through the papers inside. Was it possible she'd done her math homework and forgotten? Definitely not, and, to prove it, there was nothing inside that looked anything like the homework. Shoot.

Beside her, Caitlin had her homework laid out on her desk, ready to be corrected. Ms. Patel was on the other side of the room, going up and down the rows of desks, checking to see that everyone had completed the assignment. Natalia felt sick.

She glanced back toward Emma. Her homework was on her desk, too. Of course. Emma would *never* forget an assignment. Natalia's cousin was the most responsible kid she knew. Zoe, also, had pulled some papers out of her folder. For a moment, Natalia felt resentful. If she had known Zoe was doing her math homework, Natalia would have remembered she had to do it, too. But then she remembered that Zoe had been working right before theater club—she must have had time to do the math problems while Natalia was daydreaming about dogs and the Wicked Witch of the West.

Natalia knew she didn't have anyone but herself to blame.

Ms. Patel arrived in front of her desk. "Where's your homework, Natalia?" she asked, nicely enough.

Natalia's mouth went dry. She *always* did her homework. She didn't always do it well, but she always had something to turn in. "I forgot it," she said in a small voice.

Ms. Patel frowned. "Did you leave it at home?"

"No." Natalia gulped. "I forgot to do it."

Ms. Patel's face was stern. "Natalia," she said, softly enough that most of the class couldn't hear it, although Natalia was sure Caitlin was listening. "This isn't like you. You seem like you've been struggling in class lately, and it's really important that you keep up with homework. I expect it on my desk first thing tomorrow. If I don't see that you're catching up with the rest of the class, I'm going to email your parents about getting you some extra help."

As Ms. Patel returned to the front of the room, Natalia dropped her head down on her desk with a groan. If her parents thought she was doing badly in school, they might make her quit theater club. And they might decide taking care of the dogs was too much for her.

It wasn't fair. She could absolutely catch up. Easily. She knew it; she just needed to study a little bit. Hot tears prickled Natalia's eyes, and she quickly wiped them away before they started to fall.

Caitlin reached between their desks and squeezed Natalia's hand. "I'll tutor you if you want," she whispered.

Natalia sniffed and gave her a tiny, watery smile. "Thanks. But I'll be fine."

She knew she could bring her math grade up by herself.

⌒〜⌒

"All that for one homework assignment?" Zoe said, frowning. "It seems like she's kind of overreacting." They were standing in front of the school waiting for Emma, and Natalia had told Zoe exactly what Ms. Patel had said.

"Well . . ." Natalia said reluctantly. She could feel her cheeks getting hot. "I haven't done the best job on my homework lately. And I did pretty badly on that pop quiz she gave us last week."

"Yikes." Zoe made a face. "Want to do our homework together tonight? I can show you how to do the problems."

"I guess," Natalia said. "If we have time." She didn't really want to talk about math. She was more interested in getting to know the dogs that would be waiting for them at Seaview House.

"Maybe we can practice lines for *The Wizard of Oz* audition, too," Zoe said, her face brightening.

"Definitely," Natalia said. She felt better just thinking about it: Soon she'd be the Wicked Witch *and* she'd be making money taking care of adorable dogs. Maybe this was just the first step and soon she'd have a whole dog-walking business. She imagined herself holding three leashes in each hand, surrounded by happy puppies as she strolled through the center of town. In the daydream, she passed the old theater and saw her face, frightening in green paint, glaring out of a *Wizard of*

Oz poster. "I'll be a star *and* an entrepreneur," she said dreamily.

Zoe raised an eyebrow. "Yeah, okay," she said. "Just make sure you're a math whiz, too, superstar."

Natalia frowned. "You don't need to nag," she said. "I'll take care of it."

Emma came up to them, tightening her ponytail. She was in her soccer uniform. "Hi," she said. "Tell my mom I'll be home late, okay?"

"What's going on?" Natalia asked. "I thought you were coming on the bus."

"We're having an extra practice," Emma told them. "Coach says we need to work on our offense."

Zoe and Natalia both nodded, the way they did whenever Emma talked about soccer. Neither of them knew a thing about it. But Natalia's stomach sank. "I told my mom we'd come over to Seaview House today," she confessed. "The people who are getting married are there, and they wanted to meet us."

"Oh." Emma twisted her hands together, looking guilty. "If I'd known . . . but I have to go to practice."

She looked so sorry that Natalia hurried to reassure her. "It's okay. They just want to talk about the dogs. Zoe and I can handle it."

Zoe blew out an irritated breath. "No, we can't," she said. "If you had *told* me, I would have come, but I promised to run lines with Caitlin and some of the other kids in theater club."

"With Caitlin?" Natalia asked, surprised. "You don't even *like* Caitlin."

"That's not true," Zoe said. "Sometimes she gets on my nerves, is all. But I really want to play Dorothy, and so I need to practice before the audition." She raised an eyebrow at Natalia. "Don't you think you should come, too?"

Natalia felt a tug of longing. Practicing lines with Zoe and Caitlin and whoever else was getting together with them *did* sound like fun. Meeting the wedding couple and their dogs had sounded fun, too, but in her imaginings it had been all three of them doing it together. Doing it by herself wouldn't be as exciting. "I can't," she said regretfully. "I told Mom we'd be there."

Zoe's face softened. "If you really need me . . ." she said.

"No." Natalia shook her head firmly. Zoe wanted to be Dorothy, and Natalia wasn't going to stand in the way of that. "You're right, I should have told you guys before. I can handle it." *Meet the dogs, catch up on my math, study my lines. No sweat!*

⌒ෆ⌒

At Seaview House, Natalia's mom and Aunt Amy were seated with a couple at one of the little round brightly painted tables in the dining room. There were small plates in front of them: Natalia saw Uncle Brian's special little crab puffs on one, some kind of pasta on another, and what looked like chicken on a third.

They must be taste-testing a wedding menu, Natalia thought.

Natalia's mom grinned at her and waved her toward the table. Uncle Brian came out from the kitchen with another plate—this one had asparagus on it.

"We were thinking if we hand the hors d'oeuvres around during the cocktail hour, maybe we could go with a buffet for dinner," Aunt Amy said to the couple,

54

who were both eating the crab puffs and looked like they were enjoying them. They smiled at Natalia.

Suddenly, a big, fluffy white standard poodle popped out from under the table and put her front paws in the woman's lap, gazing beseechingly up at her.

"Not for you, Ruby!" The woman pulled her hand away, and the dog craned toward it, her frantically wagging tail jarring the table and making the glasses and dishes rattle. Aunt Amy reached out to steady the wineglasses.

"This is my daughter Natalia," Natalia's mom said. "Natalia, this is Ms. Akers and her fiancé, Mr. Cooke."

"Hi," Natalia said. "Your dog is so cute!"

"Thanks!" The woman was trying to get Ruby to put her paws on the ground, but every time she gently pushed her paws off her lap, Ruby hopped back up, licking eagerly at her hands. "She thinks she's a lapdog. You can call us Rachel and Mike."

"I thought you had two dogs, though?" Natalia asked, looking around.

"We do," Mike told her. He pointed under the table. Another big white poodle was lying calmly with his head on his paws, his eyes closed. "Bandit is the laziest dog in the world. You'd never guess he was Ruby's brother." He and Rachel both laughed.

Natalia laughed, as well. "I guess my sister and brothers and I are all pretty different, too," she said. She knelt and petted Ruby. Ruby gave up trying to climb into Rachel's lap and licked Natalia's face instead.

"Speaking of your sister, where *are* Zoe and Emma?" Aunt Amy asked. "I thought they were coming to meet Ruby and Bandit, too."

They would if I had remembered to tell them about it before they made other plans, Natalia thought guiltily. Out loud, she said, "They can't wait to meet Ruby and Bandit! But Emma had an emergency soccer practice and Zoe had to rehearse for her audition." Seeing her mom looking a little worried, she added quickly, "They'll definitely be here later to help walk Daisy and Jasper." Mentally, she made a note that she had better text them both to make sure they came.

"Well, we're so glad you and your sister and cousin can help out with Ruby and Bandit," Rachel said. "Once we check in, we're counting on you to walk the dogs for the days we're here. And you'll definitely have to look after them during the wedding." She looked at Ruby, who was now trying to get her nose on top of the table to investigate the food. "She can be a little rambunctious."

Ruby gazed at Natalia beseechingly, clearly hoping she would hand her some food. Her curly fur hung down into her big brown eyes, and Natalia's heart melted. "You're a good dog, aren't you?" she said. "We'd *love* to take care of her."

"Are Zoe and Emma on board, too?" her mother asked, looking worried. "Taking care of four dogs is too much for just one person."

"Of course!" Natalia said brightly. "They can't wait!"

Or at least that's how they'll feel once they see how lovable Ruby and Bandit are.

Chapter Five

Sunday morning, the whole family gathered at Seaview House. Uncle Brian was in the kitchen, whipping up breakfast for everyone. Everyone included the Goldsteins and the Warners, who, Natalia and Zoe's mom had told them, seemed to be enjoying their stay. When their family got to Seaview House, Natalia and Zoe headed into the kitchen to see what was cooking.

Emma was already there, nibbling a piece of bacon as her dad bent to pull something that smelled amazing out of the oven.

"Hi," she said. "Mr. Warner took the dogs out last night before bed, and I let them out for a little while this morning. But we should take them for a really long walk today."

"Definitely," Natalia said, reaching for a piece of bacon of her own.

Natalia had been walking Jasper and Daisy every day after school that past week while Emma had practice and Zoe rehearsed her audition, but she hadn't taken them out for much longer than they absolutely needed. She'd had after-school clubs a couple days—community service club and student council—and she'd had to hurry home to do her homework. Jasper and Daisy probably could use some real exercise and playtime.

"What's cooking?" Zoe asked Uncle Brian, eyeing the pan he'd just pulled out of the oven.

"French toast casserole," he said cheerfully.

"What's in it?" Natalia asked. The pan had thick slices of French toast on top, but she could see blackberries and strawberries underneath. It smelled deliciously warm and sweet.

"Oh, bread, eggs, cream, fruit, maple syrup, cinnamon," Uncle Brian said. Natalia's mouth was watering. "And we've got bacon, of course, and I'm making eggs to order. What kind would you like, Natalia? Sunny-side up? Scrambled?"

"We both like poached," Zoe told him, leaning against the counter and taking a piece of bacon off the plate that Emma was nibbling from. "But if you're making whatever eggs everyone wants, won't you be stuck in the kitchen all morning?"

Uncle Brian winked. "That's kind of my plan," he said. "I'm hiding from the guests."

Natalia frowned, confused. "You don't like them?" she asked. "I thought they were nice." The Goldsteins and the Warners were always very friendly to her, and would stop to chat whenever they saw her bringing the dogs in or out. Mrs. Goldstein went shopping every day at the little shore-town stores, buying handmade pottery mugs and chocolates and painted shells to take to all her friends at home, which Natalia thought showed what a thoughtful friend she must be, and all four of them had paid her uncle Dean to take them out on a fishing trip on his boat. He had liked them, too, which wasn't always the case with the tourists he took out.

"They're good people," Uncle Brian said. He pulled out a wooden skewer and poked it into the center of the casserole, seeing if it was done. "But it's like with the restaurant I cooked at back in Seattle. I liked the people who came there fine, but I was much happier staying out of sight and making them something tasty. I prefer that to being out front, schmoozing with them. I'm a back-of-house person."

"I think I am, too," Emma said, reaching for another piece of bacon.

Natalia thought that made sense. Emma got nervous meeting new people.

"Natalia's not, though," Emma added. "She's a front-of-house person."

"Absolutely," Uncle Brian said. He reached for a knife and began slicing the casserole. "If Natalia worked in a restaurant, she'd be the hostess or a waitress. She'd talk to everyone and make sure they were happy."

"What about me?" Zoe asked, leaning against the counter. "I don't want to talk to everyone and make them happy, but I don't want to stay in the back, either."

Natalia giggled. "You would have, like, decorated the restaurant to look really cool before it even opened."

Zoe grinned. "Nice."

Uncle Brian handed her a platter of French toast casserole slices, Natalia the dish of bacon, and Emma a basket of muffins. "Take these out, would you, girls? Sit down at a table and eat."

"Okay, thanks, Dad," Emma said.

The three girls pushed their way through the swinging doors to the dining room. It was sunny and bright, with little round tables painted in pastel colors scattered across the room. Natalia squinted against the sunlight and then followed Zoe over to the buffet to put down the bacon. Their moms had decorated the buffet table with brightly colored autumn leaves and little gourds, as well as some of the dried flowers they had been arranging.

The little tables were decorated with dried flower arrangements, too. Natalia saw the Warners and the Goldsteins sharing a pink-painted table for four and went over to say hi.

"Are you having a fun visit?" she asked.

"We are!" Mrs. Warner smiled up at her. "We're going to go down to the dinner theater in Chestertown tonight, and I can't wait!"

"That's awesome!" Natalia said. Her class had gone to the dinner theater at the end of the previous year, and she told them all about it.

"Since we're going to be out late," Mr. Goldstein added, "we were hoping you girls could take Daisy and Jasper for an extra-long walk tonight, because I'm sure we won't want to do more than let them out for a minute when we get back. We'll pay for the extra walk, of course."

"No problem!" Natalia said. She figured she could run over right before bedtime and take the dogs out. It would be easier for Emma, of course, since she lived at Seaview House, but Natalia knew Emma got up extra-early on Mondays for swim team practice before school. *I was the one who agreed to take care of the dogs, so it's my problem*, Natalia told herself, feeling a little pleased with herself for stepping up without being told.

Zoe and Emma had settled at the yellow table where Grandma Stephenson and Abuelita were splitting an omelet. Natalia took her own plate of eggs and bacon and French toast casserole and went to join them.

"The first guests' stay at the bed-and-breakfast seems to be a success," Grandma Stephenson said quietly, nodding toward the table where the Warners and Goldsteins were cheerfully finishing off some fruit.

"They're definitely having fun," Natalia agreed.

"And there'll be a lot of people here for the wedding," Emma said enthusiastically. "It's a really good start for the business."

"Speaking of good starts," Abuelita said, smiling at them. "I'm proud of how you offered to take care of the dogs. It's good for girls your age to have responsibilities."

Emma and Zoe glanced at each other, looking a little guilty, Natalia thought. It was true that they hadn't done a *ton* of dog taking-care-of, but, after all, Natalia had volunteered them without their consent. It seemed fair for her to do most of the work.

"We're going to spend all afternoon with the dogs today," Emma said, half to their grandmothers, half to Natalia.

Natalia was glad Emma and Zoe hadn't heard Mr. Goldstein asking her to take the dogs out for a late extra walk tonight. She didn't need their help, and she didn't want them feeling guilty about that, too. She could handle it herself.

⁓

"Good girl!" Natalia watched Daisy chase after the ball. "I think she's figuring it out."

"I wouldn't count on it," Zoe said, eyebrows raised, as Daisy ran past the ball and started barking up into the trees as if she expected a squirrel to pop out.

"Jasper's the smart one, aren't you, boy?" Emma said, burying her hands in Jasper's thick black fur. Jasper licked at her hands, then strolled over and picked up the ball from where it had fallen. Daisy chased after him, yapping fiercely.

"She's like Toto going after the Lion," Natalia said. "I remember that part from the movie. Now the Lion should go after her like this." She roared, running across the lawn toward the dogs. They looked at her in surprise, and then Jasper bowed playfully, his tail wagging, and ran toward her. Daisy turned in tight circles of excitement.

"Come on, Daisy-Toto." Natalia laughed. "Next, Zoe, you should slap me on the nose and tell me I should be ashamed to pick on a little dog."

"Is that part of the audition?" Emma asked as she and Zoe came over to Natalia and the dogs.

"No, the Dorothy auditions are when she first gets to Oz, and the Wicked Witch auditions are when she captures Dorothy."

"Are you both ready?" Emma asked, reaching down to pet Jasper. "They're tomorrow, right?"

"I'm totally ready," Zoe said, smiling. "Getting together with a whole group to practice a couple times really helped." She nudged Natalia. "Caitlin was actually great. I can see why you like her."

Tomorrow. Natalia hadn't exactly forgotten that auditions were on Monday, but it felt like they'd crept up on her. She'd run over lines a few times with Zoe in their bedroom, and she'd tried to study them when she had a minute, but she'd been so *busy*.

"Show me your auditions?" Emma asked, tucking her hair back behind her ear.

Zoe and Natalia hesitated. "Okay," Zoe said, her cheeks turning pink. "I know yours, too, Natalia, so let's do that one."

Zoe had memorized Natalia's audition scene as well as her own? *She must* really *be into the play*, Natalia thought.

"Sure," Natalia said. She shook out her hair so that it fluffed out witchily, and screwed up her face into an over-the-top evil expression. "Wait, I need Daisy!" She reached out and picked up Daisy, who squirmed in her arms. "Oof, she's heavy. Okay." She kissed the top of Daisy's head. "What a *nice* little dog!" she said, cackling wickedly.

It went pretty well for a while. Zoe had her lines down, and she made a good Dorothy, Natalia thought. And it was fun being the Wicked Witch. Natalia tried to loom over Zoe threateningly, which was hard because they were the same height. She bared her teeth and made her hands into claws. Emma laughed and clapped, and Jasper gazed up at her, puzzled.

But Natalia kept stumbling over her lines. "Um . . ."

she said, hesitating again after trying to take the slippers off Zoe's feet and pretending they burned her hands.

"I said, Can I still have my dog?" Zoe said. When Natalia still couldn't come up with the next line, Zoe whispered, *"Fool that I am . . ."*

"Right," Natalia said, crouching and pulling her hands back again as if she'd just discovered that the shoes wouldn't let her touch them. She made it through most of the rest of the short scene, through Toto's escape— she put Daisy down gently, and Daisy wandered off to investigate the roots of an oak tree—but then she got stuck again.

"He got away! He got away!" Zoe was putting a lot of emotion into her lines, and it seemed like she was almost sobbing with relief. Natalia absolutely could not remember what came next.

Emma began to look worried. Zoe was opening her mouth to prompt her again, and suddenly Natalia did *not* want to be prompted.

"I'll get him," she improvised in her best witchy voice. She ran a few steps after Daisy, waving her arms, pretending she was wearing a bat-like black cloak. Daisy bounced toward her excitedly. "I'll get you, my pretty," she said to the dog. "And your little *owner*, too! Mwahahahaha!" She broke out her creepiest cackle.

Emma and Zoe both laughed.

"I'm pretty sure that's not right, Natalia," Emma said. "I don't remember that from the movie at all."

"Close enough." Natalia shrugged. Zoe raised an eyebrow and started to speak, but Natalia cut her off. "I *know*, okay? Don't worry, I'll study my lines tonight."

She grinned confidently at her sister and cousin, but her shoulders felt a little tight. Usually, things came out okay, so she wasn't going to worry, but there suddenly seemed to be a lot of things she needed to do that night.

Study my lines, catch up on homework, take the dogs for a good walk . . . Natalia drew a shaky breath. It was all starting to pile up.

Chapter Six

"Are you a good witch, or a bad witch?" Caitlin whispered.

Natalia frowned at her. "Cait, you've gone through all your lines about sixteen times. Could you stop? I'm going to be saying all the Glinda lines by the time I get to my turn if you keep talking."

Caitlin looked annoyed. "Fine," she said. "I just want it to be perfect." She closed her eyes. "I'm visualizing." Her lips began to move, but she didn't make a sound. Natalia could read her lips, though: *Are you a good witch . . .*

Sighing, Natalia looked away. Everyone was nervous. The theater was buzzing with whispers as all the actors practiced their lines. Some people were too tense to sit in their seats, and there was a constant shifting and milling around.

Natalia herself didn't feel too confident. She'd read over the lines again a few times last night, but she'd just been so *tired* after finishing her homework and going to take Jasper and Daisy out for one last walk. She looked down at the script in her lap and read the lines over again several times, crooking her fingers into claws and making witchy faces. *It'll be fine,* she decided.

On Natalia's other side, Zoe sat absolutely still. She looked almost calm, but her cheeks were redder than usual, and she was holding tightly to the arms of her seat.

"You're going to be great," Natalia told her twin reassuringly.

"Please let's not talk about it," Zoe answered, staring straight ahead.

The Community Playhouse, where the kids' theater club met, was a grand old theater, with red velvet seats and elaborately carved and gilded cherubs decorating the ceiling. It had been around since the end of the nineteenth century, when traveling plays had come through Waverly for a night on their way to Baltimore and cities farther south. That didn't happen now, but the theater still saw a lot of use for everything from the high school theater program to dance recitals to kindergarten graduation. A local group put on *A Christmas Carol* for charity every year, and students from the college in Chestertown ran a summer theater festival for two weeks in June.

Natalia loved being there, loved the string of tiny dressing rooms backstage, loved standing in the wings and looking out at the audience. Even when she'd just been there to see Tomás walk across the stage with the rest of his kindergarten class last year, something about the theater itself gave Natalia a feeling of hushed, excited anticipation.

Being the Wicked Witch would be so much fun here, she thought, looking around. Finally having an important role, acting in a place where so many *real* actors had appeared over the years, would be amazing.

Ms. Andrews hopped up onstage and cleared her throat. The babble of voices quieted.

"We're going to get started with our Dorothys," she said cheerfully. "When I call your name, come on up."

Zoe stopped breathing. She was clutching the arms of her seat so tightly that her knuckles were white.

"Relax, you'll be fine," Natalia whispered.

Ms. Andrews called up the first Dorothy. She seemed like she knew her lines, but she was talking so quietly that Natalia could barely hear her.

"She's not going to get it," she whispered to Zoe. "Make sure you project when it's your turn, okay?"

"Don't speak to me," Zoe whispered back. "I can't talk or I'm going to freak out."

Natalia tried to exchange a glance with Caitlin, but Caitlin still had her eyes closed, her lips moving. Patting her sister on the arm, Natalia mimed zipping her lips with her other hand.

Zoe was the fourth girl called up to audition for Dorothy. As she watched her climb up on the stage, Natalia crossed her fingers for good luck.

After a moment, she relaxed. Zoe didn't need luck. She knew her lines, she was projecting really well, and, most of all, she sounded like she was talking, not reciting lines. She *seemed* like she was Dorothy. She even stayed in tune when she sang. Zoe was definitely the best one to audition so far.

When she came back to her seat, breathing fast and looking relieved, Natalia gave her a thumbs-up.

"At least it's over," Zoe whispered.

"Are you kidding?" Caitlin said. "You were great." Ms. Andrews shushed her from the stage, and Caitlin pursed her lips, irritated.

Natalia stared at her friend. Caitlin complimenting Zoe? They really must have started liking each other more when they were rehearsing together. She grinned to herself. Being in the play together would be so much fun, now that all three of them were friends.

She shut her eyes for a second, imagining. She and Zoe and Caitlin, side by side, taking a bow. The audience cheering. What had Caitlin said? This year was the year they were the oldest in the kids' theater group and would get the best roles. This year was their *chance*. Natalia opened her eyes and concentrated on the stage again.

None of the other prospective Dorothys were anywhere near as good as Zoe; at least that was what Natalia thought. Zoe, still looking worried, only shook her head when Natalia whispered this opinion to her.

Ms. Andrews auditioned the hopeful Scarecrows, Tin Men, and Cowardly Lions next, and Natalia went back to her script, trying to focus on getting the words perfectly if she wasn't looking. When the director called up Glindas, though, Natalia folded her script again to watch.

Several of the Glindas were fairly good. One—not Caitlin—was the best singer by far, but she mumbled during the speaking parts. Another spoke in a strange singsong voice, which might have been intentional, but Natalia didn't think it worked very well.

Caitlin was the best, in Natalia's opinion, but there were some other Glindas who were almost as good. Caitlin always put all of herself into trying to be the best at whatever she did, so she was wearing a dress that wasn't *quite* what she would usually wear to school; it was just a little fluffier and sparklier and Good Witch–looking. And she had brought a glittery toy wand and was waving it as she talked. Natalia thought what Caitlin did worked perfectly, but it was what Ms. Andrews thought that would matter.

Still, she whispered, "You were great!" when Caitlin came back to her seat, because she had been. Zoe nodded. Caitlin looked tense, but she gave them both a strained smile.

Then Natalia leaned forward intently, because Ms. Andrews had begun to call up Wicked Witches of the West.

The first four girls were . . . fine. They didn't express themselves as well as she would, Natalia thought. The Wicked Witch, in her opinion, should be over the top. She needed to cackle and snarl, and wiggle her fingers as if she were about to put a spell on Dorothy.

None of these girls did that as well as Natalia was sure *she* would. But they were okay. The one very tall girl, Darcy, who Natalia had noticed at the very first meeting—she didn't go to their school—was the best. She loomed over Ms. Andrews threateningly as Ms. Andrews read Dorothy's lines, and she twisted her face into an expression of menace.

Darcy was good, but Natalia thought she could do better. She didn't feel nervous now; she felt *excited*.

When Ms. Andrews called, "Natalia Martinez? Come on up, Natalia," Natalia felt like she was bouncing up onto the stage.

The first part of the scene went really well. Natalia cackled and crouched, made her fingers into claws, and grimaced threateningly. She could feel the other kids watching her, enjoying her performance.

Then she came to the part of the scene where she'd gotten stuck the other day. The Witch had just tried to take Dorothy's shoes off and burned her hands. Natalia hesitated. It was something about not being able to take off the slippers while Dorothy was alive. What was it, exactly?

"Can I still have my dog?" Ms. Andrews repeated.

Natalia's mouth was dry, and she swallowed hard. She looked desperately out at the other kids in the audience. Some of them were staring back at her, while others went over their lines or talked in whispers or stared off into space, daydreaming.

Then her eyes met Zoe's. Her sister was looking back at her steadily. Something about those familiar brown eyes jogged Natalia's memory. "No!" she said in a burst. "Fool that I am!"

They got a little further, through the Witch

threatening Dorothy and Toto's escape, and then Natalia got stuck again. This time, looking at Zoe didn't help. Natalia stared wildly around the stage, hoping that *something* would jog her memory. Nothing did.

"Drat you and your dog," Ms. Andrews prompted in a low voice.

"Drat you and your dog," Natalia parroted back in her best Wicked Witch voice. She had no idea what came next. But suddenly, words were spilling out of her. *Not the right words.* "Your little dog, my pretty!" she ad-libbed. "He won't get away for long! I'll send my flying monkeys after him! They got him once, they can get him again!" *This is completely wrong*, she thought. "Something wicked this way comes!" she added desperately. That wasn't from *The Wizard of Oz*, but it was definitely familiar. She gave her best witchy cackle, then looked at Ms. Andrews hopefully.

Ms. Andrews was just staring at her in surprise. Natalia didn't know what to do, so she cackled again, waving her arms in the air. *I look ridiculous*, she thought, but she couldn't stop. In the audience, someone giggled.

There was a burst of applause when she finished cackling. *Better to laugh with them than to have them laugh at me*, Natalia thought, so she gave a sweeping bow, her long hair brushing the stage, then headed for the stairs offstage.

"Thank you, Natalia," Ms. Andrews said coolly, and made a note on her clipboard. She didn't say anything else, but Natalia thought she looked disappointed.

Darcy had definitely done better in her audition than Natalia had. And the other girls who had tried out had at least remembered their lines.

Natalia knew that she had messed up. Holding her head high, she climbed down from the stage and took her seat. Caitlin nudged her and made a sympathetic face. Natalia tried to smile back, but she could feel her lips wobbling.

"You were great, except for the end," Zoe whispered. "Maybe it'll be okay."

Natalia winced. Zoe's voice was wistful, and Natalia knew her sister was trying to be encouraging. But it only made her feel worse. There was a sick, unhappy sensation in the pit of her stomach. She wiped her hand roughly across her eyes.

"I should have prepared better," she whispered back.

Natalia had thought it would be so awesome. She and her twin and her best friend, in three of the best parts in the whole play. Rehearsing together, doing each other's makeup for the show, taking a bow together, going to the cast party.

It would have been *great*, and now it wasn't going to happen. Natalia knew that with complete certainty.

I really blew it, she thought sadly.

Chapter Seven

Three days later, Natalia still couldn't think about her audition without feeling sick. She dragged her feet as she headed for Seaview House after school, the pit in her stomach deepening as she remembered the disappointed look on Ms. Andrews's face. She knew she hadn't gotten the part.

And it was all her own fault, Natalia thought, scuffing her sneakers along the sidewalk. She had just *assumed* the audition would be fine. She should have rehearsed and rehearsed like Zoe and Caitlin had.

While Zoe was still in the shower that morning, their mom had told Natalia that the wedding party would be checking in today with Ruby and Bandit. After school, the girls would need to start taking care of all four dogs. Natalia knew her mom expected her to let Zoe and

Emma know, but she hadn't told them. It wasn't Zoe's fault Natalia had blown the audition, but Zoe had done *so* well, and Natalia had done *so* badly. Natalia didn't want to be around her sister right now.

And Natalia was the one who had agreed to take care of the dogs. She might not have practiced hard enough for her audition, and she might not be doing great in math right now, but she *was* a responsible person, she thought, tears stinging the backs of her eyes again. She could handle the dogs.

Natalia slowed even more as she approached Seaview House. The sun was shining and the last of the roses were still blooming on the bushes in front of the house. Several cars were parked out front. As Natalia watched, a woman she didn't know climbed out of one of the cars, her arms full of golden fabric, and hurried into the house.

Usually, Natalia liked meeting new people. But right now, the idea made her very tired. Still, she steeled herself and lifted her chin, putting a smile on her face. She *was* going to keep her promises and take care of all four dogs, and she would be nice to everyone she saw. She *was* responsible.

Inside, Seaview House was buzzing with activity. Aunt Amy and a woman who looked like an older version of Rachel-the-bride were hanging the golden fabric, draping it across the back wall of the dining room.

"And gold tablecloths," the woman was saying. "Will there be enough white flowers?"

"We have enough white roses left in the gardens to make the arrangements they want on the tables," Aunt Amy told her. "And the florist will be here first thing on Saturday for the arrangements for the ceremony."

The woman—*Rachel's mom?* Natalia thought—nodded in satisfaction and tucked the fabric she was holding to the wall with a long pin.

"Hi!" Aunt Amy said cheerfully to Natalia. "Rosemary, this is my niece Natalia. She and her sister and my daughter are taking care of the dogs. Natalia, this is Mrs. Akers, Rachel's mom."

"Hello, dear," the woman said. "I hope you can handle them. Why Rachel and Mike are insisting on having those dogs in the wedding party I have no idea."

Natalia smiled politely. "They're nice dogs," she said. "I can manage them."

"Bandit and Ruby are upstairs in their owners' sitting room," Aunt Amy said briskly. "Jasper and Daisy are out on the screened porch."

Rachel's mom frowned. "There are other dogs?" she said worriedly. "Ruby's a handful."

"It's okay, I've got this," Natalia said, trying to project confidence.

"And it's not just her," Aunt Amy said reassuringly. "Where are the others, Natalia?"

Natalia waved vaguely back toward the door. "Outside," she said. "We're fine." *And I'm not lying*, she thought defiantly. *They're outside of Seaview House, even if they're not* right *outside. And we* are *fine.*

Aunt Amy and Rachel's mother began discussing decorating again, and Natalia took the opportunity to head for the stairs. The clatter of pots and pans and the sound of more voices showed that Uncle Brian was in the kitchen with at least a few more guests. As Natalia started up the stairs, another older couple hurried past, followed by a younger woman.

She smiled at them politely, but it was a relief when the noise died down and Natalia was alone upstairs.

Rachel and Mike had the nicest suite of rooms on this floor, the one Natalia's mom and Aunt Amy called the "honeymoon suite": a big bedroom that overlooked the garden, and a bathroom that had a giant claw-foot tub and a totally separate walk-in shower. Best of all was the sitting room, which had a floor painted to look like a medieval map, with odd-shaped continents and an illustration of a puff-cheeked cloud-man blowing a boat across a blue-green sea. Natalia's great-grandfather had painted it more than seventy years ago, when Grandma Stephenson was just a baby, and every few years, she would hire a local artist to come in and carefully trace over the paint, so that the colors stayed vibrant and beautiful.

It was the best part of the whole suite, better than the view of the garden and the fancy bathtub. Well, usually it was. When Natalia opened the sitting room door, she saw that somebody had lugged down an old carpet, a ragged blue-and-gold one Natalia vaguely recognized from the attic, and had spread it out to cover the floor from wall to wall.

A warm, furry body slammed into her, making her

stagger backward, and she realized why the rug was there. Ruby was practically bouncing off the walls. If the rug hadn't been there, the whole floor would probably have been scratched up by dog nails as she paced around.

"Hey there, pretty girl," Natalia said, dropping to her knees so that she could rumple Ruby's ears and pet her. "You lonely? You need a good run?" Ruby's tail beat the air as she licked Natalia's face, wiggling with delight. "Yuck, yucky kiss," Natalia said to her in a baby voice, wiping off the dog spit, but she didn't really mind. "Where's Bandit, huh?"

She pushed Ruby gently backward so that she could get farther into the room. Bandit was sprawled in the middle of the rug. Without raising his head from the carpet, he thumped his tail twice, then closed his eyes.

With dismay, Natalia saw there were scraps of chewed paper everywhere, scattered across the rug, even on the seats of the chairs. "Did you do this, Ruby?" Natalia asked, picking one piece gingerly off a chair between the tips of two fingers. "Bad girl." Ruby, undiscouraged, panted up at her happily.

The paper, she saw, was a scrap of newspaper. All the others looked like they were, too. "That's a relief," Natalia muttered. "At least you didn't chew up anything important." She crawled around the room on her knees, gathering up scraps of paper. Ruby, apparently deciding this was a delightful new game, followed behind her, occasionally making a whuffing noise and trying to lick Natalia's face. Bandit cracked an eye open and watched them for a couple minutes before closing his eyes again.

"There," she said finally, tossing the handful of ruined newspaper in the trash. "I think that was pretty *responsible* of me, don't you, Ruby?" Ruby barked, and Natalia patted her again. "I'm glad you agree. Let's go."

She took the dogs' leashes off the sideboard, and Ruby almost exploded with joy, whipping around in ecstatic circles so that Natalia had to catch her to get the leash on. Finally, Ruby was properly leashed and Natalia bent and snapped the second leash to Bandit's collar. "Come on, good boy," she said as he slowly heaved himself to his feet. "You can do it."

Natalia's mom looked up as they hurried down the stairs, Ruby straining at the leash and Bandit yawning and walking as slowly as he could manage while still being with Ruby and Natalia. She frowned slightly, a little anxious line appearing between her eyebrows. "You okay, honey?" she asked.

"Sure!" Natalia said brightly. She was relieved to be all the way down without having fallen on the stairs. "I've just got to get Daisy and Jasper."

Her mom shook her head. "Four dogs is a lot at once. I'm glad you've got Zoe and Emma to help you."

"Yup," Natalia said, heading for the door. *I'm not lying*, she told herself. *Zoe and Emma are helping me. Just not right now.*

Outside, it was cooler, and late-afternoon shadows were starting to spread across the grass. Natalia hadn't realized picking up the paper had taken so much time. "We'd better get the other dogs, huh?" she said to Ruby and Bandit. "I bet they want a nice long walk, too."

Keeping a firm hold on the leash so that Ruby wouldn't dash away, Natalia led the dogs across the wide front lawn and around the corner of Seaview House, toward the screened back porch, where Daisy and Jasper were waiting.

As they got closer, Natalia could hear Daisy yapping. "She probably sees a squirrel," she told Ruby and Bandit. "Daisy loves squirrels."

Ruby stiffened and stopped. She glared at the screened-in porch, her lips curling back to show her teeth. "What's going on, girl?" Natalia asked.

With a sudden jerk, Ruby began to stalk forward across the grass, dragging Natalia and Bandit after her. When she got just a few feet from the screened porch, she stopped and barked twice. Low, threatening barks, nothing like the happy barks of excitement Natalia had heard from her before. Daisy and Jasper stared back at her and then Daisy scuttled to the farthest end of the porch and hid under a swing. Jasper charged forward and began barking deep, loud barks back at Ruby.

"Okay, no," Natalia said. "Hush. Ruby, hush. Jasper! Quiet!"

Jasper paused for a moment, but Ruby continued to snarl and bark, glaring at the dogs on the screened porch. In response, Jasper began to bark again. Daisy, huddled beneath the swing, began to yap nervously, too. Bandit ignored all of them and sniffed at the grass.

"No!" Natalia said again. "Stop it!" She pulled Ruby back around the corner of the house, Ruby straining at the leash and barking at Jasper the whole way.

As soon as they got around the corner, Ruby's angry glare disappeared and her tail went back up. She panted up at Natalia as if to say, *What's up? Aren't we going to play?* Bandit sighed and sniffed at a bush.

"I see," Natalia said to Ruby. "Is that how you're going to be?" Ruby put her front paws on Natalia's legs and tried to reach high enough to lick her face. Natalia wasn't happy—how was she supposed to walk the dogs if she couldn't get them near each other?—but Ruby was so sweet that she could feel her heart softening.

Experimentally, she led the dogs back toward the corner of the house. As soon as they came in sight of the screened porch where Jasper and Daisy were, Ruby began to snarl. Natalia pulled her and Bandit back to the side lawn. Immediately, Ruby appeared to forget about the other dogs once more.

Natalia groaned and closed her eyes. "This is not ideal," she said to the dogs. Ruby yipped happily.

Opening her eyes again, Natalia frowned at the bay out beyond Seaview House's gardens. Sunlight gleamed off the water, but long shadows were spreading, too. It was almost dinnertime. There was no way she could take both sets of dogs for good walks separately, have dinner, and get her homework done before bedtime. Not without help.

I should be able to do this by myself, she thought. *But maybe, just this once, it would be more responsible to ask for help.*

Her cell phone was in a zippered pocket on the inside of her jacket. Switching both leashes to her left hand, she pulled it out and stared down at it. *Zoe or Emma?* Either of them would come help her if she really needed them, she knew.

She didn't want to ask Zoe right now. Emma had a rare Friday game after school tomorrow, but at least she hadn't witnessed Natalia's humiliation at theater club. Emma didn't even know about it. Making up her mind, Natalia called Emma.

It took Emma a couple rings to pick up. "Natalia?" she asked. "I'm at my study group. Do you want to come over?" She dropped her voice so that she was almost whispering. "We could work on your math."

Natalia winced. She had been carefully *not* thinking about the fact that she still didn't understand what they were doing in math class. Still, she couldn't worry about that now. *I'll catch up before the test,* she thought optimistically.

"I can't," she said. "Emma, can you leave? I kind of need your help."

Emma's study group was meeting at a house less than ten minutes away, and she hurried over. Natalia had known she would; Emma would do anything to help Natalia or Zoe.

"How come you didn't tell me that the wedding dogs were coming today?" Emma asked, petting Bandit. "Does Zoe know?"

Natalia adjusted Ruby's leash so she didn't have to look up at her cousin. "Oh, you guys are busy," she said casually. "And I didn't think I needed help. I wouldn't have if Ruby wasn't being such a weirdo about the other dogs. I'll tell Zoe tonight." She led Ruby around the corner and Ruby began to snarl again as soon as Jasper and Daisy came into sight.

"She's very fierce, isn't she?" Emma said.

"I just don't understand it," Natalia said mournfully. "She's so nice to *people*."

"Oh, well," Emma said, sounding resigned. "You take her and Bandit this way and down toward the park, and I'll take Daisy and Jasper toward the water. I'll grab a ball or something and play catch with them. We'd better hurry before it gets dark."

"Okay," Natalia agreed. With a surge of affection, she reached out and squeezed her cousin's hand. "Thanks a lot, Emma. I'm really glad you could come."

Emma shrugged, smiling. "No problem. We'll get it done a lot faster with two of us."

She headed off toward the screened porch, and Natalia led Ruby and Bandit toward the front of the house. She couldn't help knowing that they would have gotten it done even faster with three. *I don't want Zoe to know I couldn't do this alone,* she thought. *Not right now. Not after the audition.*

That night, Natalia stared down at her math book and sighed. Zoe was already asleep, the covers pulled over her head so that there was only a huddled lump visible in her bed. Once Zoe climbed into bed, that was it. She was practically a champion sleeper.

Natalia's eyes felt heavy and dry with sleepiness, and her arms ached from holding Ruby back and tugging Bandit forward for the entire long walk. She had meant to do her homework earlier, but she had been late getting home for dinner. Her mom was still at Seaview House, organizing stuff for the wedding, and her dad had asked if she and Zoe could watch Tomás and Mateo while he graded his high school students' papers. Natalia had lost track of time while she played with her little brothers.

She'd sat down to her homework late. She'd read a story and answered questions for English, and she'd done her science and social studies. But she had saved the math for last, and now she was so tired.

I should have done the math first because it's hardest, Natalia thought guiltily. *I didn't want to, but that's not an excuse. And now I just want to sleep.*

She tried to focus on the first problem, but the numbers were fuzzy. Nothing made sense. *Find* x, *find* y, she thought, looking at the page with dislike. *I'm going to get these all wrong anyway.*

With a sigh, Natalia closed the book and reached for her pajamas.

I'll catch up tomorrow.

Chapter Eight

"Go, Emma!" Natalia and Zoe whooped and cheered as Emma dodged one of her opponents and kicked a long pass to her teammate Vivian. "Good job!" Natalia shouted as Emma dropped back, waiting for the ball to travel back to her side of the field. Emma heard, and shot her a quick smile before returning her attention to the field, poised to leap back into action.

"Why isn't she running after the ball?" Natalia asked, leaning against their dad, who was watching the game intently.

"Because she has to stay in her position," her dad said, tugging at the end of her ponytail. "They can't just dash all over the field."

Natalia shrugged. "That's how we play it at recess."

"Who cares, anyway?" Zoe said, inspecting her fingernails. "We only come to watch Emma."

Their dad shook his head, but he was smiling. "It's shameful," he said. "If only my dad, your *abuelo*, could hear you. He loved *fútbol*. When I was a little kid, he'd take me to games and put me up on his shoulders so I could watch. Sometimes we'd hang out after and get the players' autographs."

"It sounds like fun," Natalia said, trying to picture her dad as a little kid, perched on his dad's shoulders above the crowd. It was hard to imagine: Her dad was solid and tall, built like a wall. Natalia had heard from friends of hers with older siblings that some of the high school students he taught were intimidated by him, until they got to know him and realized how kind he was. It was typical of him that he came straight to Emma's after-school game after a long day of teaching.

Someone kicked the ball back toward Emma and she sprang into action, dribbling quickly down the field. One of the other players tried to take the ball from her, but she dodged her neatly. Zoe stuck two fingers in her mouth and whistled, loud and shrill.

"Em-MA! Em-MA!" Natalia chanted, and added, "Go, sports!" Her dad snorted and rolled his eyes, grinning.

When Emma had passed the ball again and the action moved downfield, Natalia returned to the subject of her grandfather. "I guess Abuelo would have liked Emma, huh?" she asked. "Even though she isn't his granddaughter, he would have been proud that she was so good at soccer."

Her dad wrapped his arms around her and Zoe's shoulders, pulling them close. "Of course Abuelo would have liked Emma," he said. "Who wouldn't like Emma? But he would have been so proud of you girls, too."

"Yeah?" Natalia nestled closer, feeling warm inside.

"Absolutely. You girls are kind and funny and talented and smart, and you both do well in school. He would have spent half his time bragging about you to all the other old men at the *fútbol* games."

Her dad squeezed them both, one in each arm, before he let them go, but Natalia didn't feel warm and cozy anymore. At the mention of doing well in school, a chill filled her stomach and began to spread through her body. *I forgot to do my math homework*, she thought. *Again.*

She'd left yesterday's homework undone and, feeling hot with embarrassment and uncomfortably guilty, had lied to Ms. Patel, telling her it was finished, just forgotten at home. She'd felt Zoe's surprised gaze on her back the whole time Zoe knew Natalia hadn't done her homework, and she would never expect her to lie about it—and she wasn't sure if Ms. Patel had believed her, either. Natalia had promised to bring the assignment in on Monday, but there had been tight lines around her teacher's mouth that made her think she was rapidly running out Ms. Patel's patience.

And now she had two math assignments to do over the weekend.

She'd meant to get as much as she could done in the time between when school ended and when Emma's game began, but instead she'd daydreamed about the wedding, imagining Ruby and Bandit walking together down the aisle, heads held high, perfectly behaved, bearing the rings tied to giant golden bows around their necks.

Now that she thought about it again, the "perfectly behaved" part seemed a little unlikely.

She'd make sure Emma and Zoe came with her to walk the dogs today so that she could get done in plenty of time to concentrate on her homework, she decided.

A whistle blew, and the teams scattered, gathering in their own groups. Emma and her teammates were hugging and high-fiving.

"Is it over?" Zoe asked, watching them line up to shake hands with the other team.

"Emma's team won, right?" Natalia checked, and her dad nodded.

"Hey!" Emma ran off the field and over to them.

"Emma!" Natalia said, hugging her. "Great game!"

"Yes, really terrific," Zoe added. "Good job!"

Emma looked at them for a long moment, the corners of her mouth tilting up knowingly. "Uh-huh. What was your favorite part?" she asked.

Natalia and Zoe looked at each other. "When you kicked the ball?" Natalia said at last.

"Thanks for coming, you guys," Emma said, grinning

at them affectionately. "I really appreciate you showing up." She turned to Natalia and Zoe's dad. "What did *you* think, Uncle Luis?"

"You played very well," he told her, patting her shoulder. "You're getting a lot of control over the ball, and a lot of strength in your kick. You'll be a shoo-in for the high school team in a couple years."

Emma blushed. "You think so? Thanks," she said, looking suddenly shy. Then she cleared her throat and turned to Natalia and Zoe. "Let me change out of my uniform and we'll go walk the dogs."

"Great!" Natalia said, clapping her hands. "Let's see some hustle, soccer star! We've got things to do!"

ᘓᘐ

Natalia rubbed her left hand over the one holding Ruby's leash. The temperature had dipped lower since Emma's soccer game. All the leaves on the beech tree in front of the house were bright gold now—she'd heard her mom say they'd look nice in the wedding pictures—and the leaves rattled drily together as the brisk wind blew through them. Something about the coldness of the air and knowing the other girls were just around the corner with the other dogs made her feel lonely.

"It'll be more fun to walk dogs together instead of splitting up," she called. "Let's see how close we can get before Ruby freaks out."

Zoe peeked around the corner. "I have trouble believing she's as bad as you say. She's such a nice dog."

"Nice with *people*." Emma's voice came from out of sight. "Wait until you see."

Slowly, Zoe led Daisy into sight. The transformation in Ruby was immediate. Her ears went back and she charged forward, growling.

"Yikes!" Zoe said, and disappeared back around the corner, a frightened Daisy leading the way.

"Told you," Emma said. "We'd better split up like we did yesterday."

"Nooooo," Natalia complained, making her voice extra-whiny. "I want to hang out with you guys." Walking Ruby and Bandit by herself yesterday while Emma walked Daisy and Jasper in the opposite direction had been a lot less fun than it would have been to walk the dogs together. "Tell you what," she suggested. "I'll put Ruby on the porch and walk the other dogs with you guys, and then I'll walk her by herself later." It would take longer, but spending the extra time with Zoe and Emma would be worth it.

She led Ruby to the porch and shut her in. Ruby whined, her head cocked to one side as if she were saying, *What's going on? That wasn't much of a walk!*

"It's your own fault," Natalia told her. "You need to learn to play well with others." Ruby whined again, putting her nose against the screen of the porch, and Natalia patted her through the screen. "Don't worry. You'll get your turn soon." Ruby barked as Natalia walked away, turning the corner of the house to find the others.

"I can take Ruby out later," Emma offered, handing her Jasper's leash. "It'll be easier for me because I live here, and I don't have anything else I have to do tonight." They walked down toward the water, skirting around the gardens, which were taking on their fall shades of brown and yellow, since only fall flowers and a few roses were left.

"It's my responsibility," Natalia argued, feeling

vaguely guilty. "I'm the one who said we'd take care of the dogs."

"I don't mind," Emma said. "I like Ruby."

"Okay," Natalia said. "Thanks!" She felt lighter suddenly: She hadn't wanted to *ask* the others to help with the dogs, but it was a relief that she didn't have to stay all afternoon. She wanted to get her math homework done before the weekend started so she wouldn't have to worry about it anymore. "Let's race," she suggested. "Jasper, you're the fastest, aren't you, my good boy?"

"Hey, no fair," Zoe objected. "You've got the fastest dog."

"No excuses!" Natalia said, laughing. "Last one to the beach is a rotten egg!" Jasper began to trot alongside her, and she sped up more, encouraging him to run.

They reached the beach well before the others. Daisy's legs were too short to keep up, and Bandit dawdled. Natalia ran back and forth at the water's edge, her sneakers getting wet and Jasper dashing along beside her, snapping at the waves and giving deep, happy barks.

"Look at that," she said when Zoe and Emma and the other dogs caught up. "Jasper loves the water."

"Let's find some driftwood for him to chase," Zoe said, unfastening Daisy's leash and letting her loose to dash off after seagulls.

"Not actually *into* the water, though," Emma said worriedly. "It's too cold."

"Don't worry," Natalia said, feeling lighthearted. Emma was such a worrier. Natalia spotted a likely-looking piece of wood down near the waterline and ran to grab it before the waves washed it out again. "Come on, boy," she called to Jasper, and threw the stick to Zoe. "Can you get it?"

Jasper barked and ran after it, making a U-turn when Zoe threw the stick to Emma. Daisy abandoned the seagull chase to dart after him, her short legs churning up the sand so that it tangled in the fur on her belly.

I'll have to brush that out before I can start on my home-work, Natalia thought, then shook off the thought. She could save that problem for later and just have fun now.

Daisy yipped and rolled on the sand. Jasper leaped into the air and finally caught the driftwood, and Zoe ran after him, trying to get it back. Bandit, flat on his belly on the beach, sighed and shut his eyes.

After they'd worn themselves out playing keep-away with Jasper, the girls clipped the dogs' leashes back on. "Come on, sleepy boy," Emma said, tugging on Bandit's leash. "I've got to take your sister out before it gets dark. You can come, too. A second walk! What a lucky boy!"

"I . . . really don't think that will be a treat for him," Natalia said, watching Bandit reluctantly pad along. She looked up and caught Zoe eyeing her. "What? Is there sand on my face?"

"No," Zoe replied. "I was just wondering what you're going to do when we get home."

"I don't know," Natalia told her. "Have a snack, do my homework. Maybe watch some TV. What do you want to do?"

"I think you should really concentrate on your homework," Zoe said, frowning. "Especially math."

"I said I was going to do homework, didn't I?" Natalia said. Why was Zoe nagging her about this? She was her sister, not her *mom*.

"Are you *really* okay in math?" Zoe asked abruptly. "Like, once you have time to do your missing homework, you won't have any more problems? You understand what you're doing?"

"Of course I do," Natalia snapped. She was starting to feel hot and aggravated. Why did Zoe have to ruin their nice afternoon by *talking* about this?

"Oh, yeah?" Zoe said. She looked mad now, too, her nose scrunched with annoyance. "How about this? If $2x - 4 = 8$, then what does x equal?"

"I *don't care*," Natalia said, glaring at her sister.

Zoe ran in front of Natalia to block her way, yanking Daisy along with her. "*I* care," she said. "If Mom and Dad find out you're flunking math, they'll make you quit the theater club. And it won't be anywhere near as much fun without you."

"I'm *not flunking math*," Natalia nearly shouted. There was a hot feeling burning in the middle of her chest.

"It's a pretty easy problem once you understand it," Emma said quietly behind them. "See, if you add the four to both sides—"

Natalia whirled on her. "I don't need your help!" she said through gritted teeth. Emma's face fell, and Natalia immediately felt bad.

Before she could apologize for snapping at Emma, who had only been trying to help, Zoe broke in, her face red with frustration and anger. "You don't need help? That's a laugh!" she said. "You needed Emma's help yesterday to walk the dogs. You need her help again today, because it's too much for you, even though you're the one who promised we'd take care of them. You should have asked for my help for the audition, and *obviously* you need our help with math."

Natalia felt like she was going to cry, but instead she glared at her sister. "Fine," she said. "Fine. If that's the way you feel about me, *you* don't have to do anything. I don't remember asking for your help with anything. And you guys agreed to take care of the dogs, too."

"After you'd already promised for us," Zoe muttered.

"Stop it, you guys," Emma said loudly. Zoe and Natalia both turned to look at her in surprise. Emma usually didn't raise her voice. Bandit, Daisy, Jasper, and Emma were all staring at them, Natalia saw, and they all wore the same expression of alert anxiety.

"You're saying things you don't mean," Emma told them. "Natalia, Zoe's just frustrated because she wants to make sure you're okay. And, Zoe, you're hurting Natalia's feelings, and that's the last thing you want to do."

The sisters stared at each other for a moment. "Come on," Emma said coaxingly. "You know I'm right."

Zoe's lips turned up in a tiny, reluctant smile. "I didn't really mean to blow up at you," she said. "I'm sorry."

"Whatever," Natalia said, still feeling hurt. Zoe's smile disappeared, and Natalia looked away. There was a sick, empty feeling inside her. Zoe thought Natalia couldn't handle stuff, thought she needed help to handle her audition and her commitments. As she turned to walk on, Jasper tugging lightly at the leash, one thought ran through Natalia's mind.

I'm not going to ask them for help again. Either of them. I'll do it on my own.

Chapter Nine

On Monday, Natalia stifled a yawn as she dug through her folder for her math homework. She'd spent all weekend walking the dogs, playing with the dogs, and cleaning up after the dogs—she was more tired than she'd ever been before. Her eyelids felt heavy with weariness, and all morning she had dragged her feet down the hall from class to class, her teachers' words mostly only a buzz in her ears.

Natalia wasn't used to feeling this way, and she didn't like it.

"Are you okay?" Caitlin asked, pausing in her routine of lining up the pencils on her desk.

"Totally fine," Natalia said, fixing a bright smile on her face. "Sleepy, I guess."

At least she'd gotten all her math homework assignments done. She'd struggled over them Sunday night and finally scrawled what were almost definitely the wrong answers. Natalia had been able to feel Zoe watching her from across the room, but had been absolutely unwilling to ask her for help. But the important thing was having something to turn in.

Natalia pulled out the papers and handed them to Ms. Patel, getting an approving smile in return. *She won't look so pleased after she grades them*, Natalia thought.

Relieved to have handed her stuff in, Natalia leaned forward as Ms. Patel moved toward the whiteboard. She was determined to pay close attention. Whatever Zoe thought, Natalia was sure she could figure out the math herself, if she just tried hard enough. It was true, she'd been so busy she hadn't paid enough attention, but now that was going to change.

"Okay, class," Ms. Patel said cheerfully, picking up a dry-erase marker. "Today we're going to review how we write a word problem as an algebraic equation, and then we're going to solve the equations to get our answers." She wrote on the board. "Say that Jessica has eleven sets of . . ."

She kept talking, and Natalia honestly tried to listen. But she was *so* tired. Her head felt heavier and heavier and it drooped forward on her neck, her eyelids falling . . .

Suddenly, a sharp elbow jabbed into her side. Natalia jerked upright, her heart pounding hard. Confused, she looked at Caitlin, who had pulled her elbow back and was gazing studiously at the board.

"Do you know the answer, Natalia?" Ms. Patel sounded irritated, as if this wasn't the first time she had asked the question.

"Six?" Natalia guessed, saying the first thing that popped into her head.

"Very good." Ms. Patel turned to the other side of the classroom. "Dan, could you explain how Natalia got that answer?"

Natalia flopped back in her chair, incredulous. A warm tingle spread through her chest and down through her arms to her fingers. For the rest of class, she floated along, basking in her own good luck.

$\backsim\hspace{-0.3em}\backsim$

By the time she got to the cafeteria for lunch, Natalia had woken up a bit more, but she still felt tired and hollow. She made her way between the tables full of chattering kids, feeling like it was taking a lot more effort than usual, and sat down next to Emma at their usual lunch table.

"Good job in math today," Emma said casually, peeking into her lunch tote.

Natalia ducked her head, embarrassed. It had been amazing to guess the right answer without even hearing the question in class, but she felt weird hearing Emma's praise.

"Let's see what my dad packed for us today," Emma said, wiggling her eyebrows.

Since Uncle Brian had left the restaurant in Seattle where he had been head chef and come out to cook at Seaview House, Natalia hadn't bought a single lunch in the cafeteria. He made amazing food, and he always packed enough for all three of them. Zoe and a couple of her friends had started sitting with them instead of at their own table, lured over by Uncle Brian's food.

"I'm starving," Zoe said now, slipping into a seat

across the table next to her friend Ava. She and Natalia exchanged a glance, but neither said anything about math class or walking the dogs. They'd been avoiding the subjects since their argument, and Natalia was glad. She hated fighting with Zoe. *And I don't need her thinking I can't handle things myself,* she thought.

"Okay," Emma said, pulling neat little containers of food out of the tote. "Today we have individual quiches made with chanterelle mushrooms and leeks."

"Ooh, yum," Natalia said, opening a box to find the tiny eggy dish, its crust golden brown. She loved Uncle Brian's quiches. They were tender enough to melt in her mouth, with just a little crispness from the crust.

"And?" Zoe asked expectantly.

Emma opened another container. "Avocado, mango, and strawberry salad," she announced. "And I know there are big chocolate chip cookies for dessert, because I helped make them yesterday."

"I love mangoes," Zoe commented, reaching for a fork.

Ava stared at them. "Your lunches are always so weird," she said. "I can't decide if they sound good, but they're definitely more interesting than mine." She waved half of her peanut butter and jelly at them, then let it flop back onto her napkin.

"You can try a bite of this," Zoe offered, and then looked up as Caitlin came to a halt by their table. Instead of sitting down in her regular seat, she stood poised, obviously with something important to say.

"What's up?" Natalia asked.

Caitlin widened her eyes and spoke slowly and with great emphasis. "The cast list is up."

Natalia's breath caught and she pressed her hands against her chest. *I didn't make it. I couldn't have made it. Ms. Andrews hated my audition,* she thought, all very quickly. But she couldn't help hoping, just a little bit. "And?" she asked.

"I made it." Caitlin grinned a huge, sparkling grin. "I'm going to be Glinda."

Natalia jumped up and hugged her. "That's so great! Congratulations!"

"Thanks!" Caitlin hugged her back, but when they let go of each other, she had stopped smiling. "But, um . . ."

"I didn't get the Wicked Witch, did I?" Natalia asked, and Caitlin shook her head. Natalia swallowed hard, once, and then forced another smile onto her face. It felt a lot stiffer than the one from a couple minutes before, but it was there. "Oh, well," she said. "I figured that. I mean, I totally blew the audition, didn't I?" She laughed a little, awkwardly.

Caitlin smoothed her skirt over her hips and sat down. "Next year," she said. "You're in the cast, though—you should check it out."

Natalia looked over toward the far end of the cafeteria, where a small crowd was congregating around the cast list. The last thing she wanted to do was worm her way through to look at the list in front of everyone who had seen her blow the audition. She was probably, like, a flying monkey or something. "Just tell me."

Caitlin took a sip of her juice before answering. "You're Second Apple Tree," she said finally.

Second Apple Tree? That was worse than a flying monkey.

Emma patted her on the shoulder. "I'm sorry. But that'll be fun, right? You'll get to throw apples at Dorothy."

"Sure," Natalia muttered. "Who got the Witch?"

"Darcy Williams," Caitlin said. "She's that tall girl?"

Zoe had been looking back and forth between them throughout the whole conversation, and she finally broke in. "What about me? Did I get Dorothy?"

Caitlin looked thoughtful. "Hmm," she said, tapping a long finger against her chin. "I'm sorry, I didn't notice. You'd better go see."

Zoe huffed a frustrated breath through her nose as she stood up. She hurried off toward the cast list. Caitlin grinned.

"You totally know if she got it or not," Natalia realized.

"Of course I do," Caitlin said, a smile still lurking at the corners of her mouth. "She'll be more excited if sees it herself. She's going to be Dorothy."

Natalia swallowed again. It felt like there was a hard lump in the back of her throat. "That's great," she said, forcing a cheerful tone into her voice. Both Caitlin and Emma were looking at her worriedly, but Natalia went on, smiling broadly. "She worked really hard. She absolutely deserves it."

And it was true. Zoe had worked really hard, and

Natalia hadn't. Zoe deserved to get the part she wanted, and Natalia didn't. Natalia was even happy for Zoe, mostly. Her sister was going to make a great Dorothy.

But Natalia still really, really wished she had gotten the part of the Wicked Witch.

Chapter Ten

"It's not like I'm not happy for Zoe and Caitlin," Natalia said, keeping a firm hold on Daisy's leash as the little dog tried to charge across the lawn after a squirrel.

"I know," Emma said comfortingly. Jasper was being good, trotting along obediently at her side.

"It's just . . ." Natalia let her voice trail off. She knew that Emma knew what she meant. It was hard to watch her sister and her friend be so happy about their important parts, even though they deserved them, when she had blown her own audition.

"Yeah, I understand how you feel," Emma told her. "You would have made a great Wicked Witch."

"Yeah," Natalia agreed. There was a sharp ache in the center of her chest. It was *humiliating* to have such a small part, when her twin and her friend had some of the biggest parts in the show, but she didn't want to actually say that.

"We'd better head back to catch the bus," she said instead, looking up at the sky. It was still tinted with early-morning pink, but the sun was well above the horizon now. Out on the bay, line after line of waves broke, white-tipped, and washed toward the shore. Small white boats scudded, their sails puffed out by the wind. "Thanks for walking Ruby and Bandit earlier." Emma had gotten up at dawn to walk the first pair of dogs so that Natalia could sleep just a little longer, and Natalia appreciated it. She didn't feel as fuzzy-minded and sleepy as she had the day before.

"No problem," Emma said. "I can't help after school, though. I have practice."

"It's okay," Natalia said, tugging Daisy gently around to head back toward Seaview House. "Zoe said she'd help before theater club." Now that the the show had been cast, they were meeting more often.

Both Emma and Zoe had volunteered to take turns walking the dogs without Natalia having to ask them. Natalia suspected that they had noticed how sleepy and distracted she was in school the day before and thought she needed their help. She still felt a hot resentment at the things Zoe had said, and she wouldn't have *asked* them for help, but she couldn't help admitting to herself that it was nice to have them both pitching in.

❧

All day at school, Natalia felt bright and alert, the way she was *used* to feeling but hadn't felt lately.

"Hey!" Zoe said, catching up to her in the hall near the end of the day. "How's it going? Where were you at lunch?"

The slight distance she'd felt from Zoe since the cast list went up didn't seem to matter right then, not after the good day she'd been having, and Natalia smiled at her. "Ava and Caitlin and I had a service club leaders' meeting," she said. "We need to start planning the canned food drive."

"Cool, count me in for helping with the collection." Zoe smoothed her bob, tucking the ends of her hair neatly behind her ears. "Listen, I know I said I would come walk the dogs before theater club, but now a couple of us are supposed to come early to run over some songs."

"Oh." Natalia thought for a minute. She had to be at theater club by 4:30. She'd be home by 3:15, would have to drop off her bag and walk over to Seaview House, which would probably take her until almost 3:30. It would take her twenty minutes to walk to the theater from Seaview House, so she needed to finish with the dogs by ten after four. Maybe she could eat a snack while she walked the dogs.

Zoe was beginning to look uncomfortable. "Is that okay? I mean, maybe I could explain to Ms. Andrews that I have to be late. If you need me. I know it takes a while to walk both pairs of dogs, but I figured Emma would help."

Natalia remembered Zoe saying, *You don't need help? That's a laugh!* and smiled, gritting her teeth. "No, it's totally fine," she said brightly. "Emma and I will do it together."

❧

At 4:55, Natalia rushed into the theater, panting from running most of the way from Seaview House. Bandit had dragged his feet during his and Ruby's walk, while Daisy had pulled her leash out of Natalia's hand so she could chase squirrels, and it had taken Natalia more than five minutes to catch her.

And then her mom had stopped her as Natalia was hurrying to take the dogs back to their rooms. "They'd like you to be here all day on the day of the wedding," she said. "Check with the other girls, okay?" Natalia had reassured her that it would be fine. *I'll have to make sure Emma and Zoe are free on Saturday,* she reminded herself.

On the stage, Zoe, the girl who was playing the Cowardly Lion, the boys who were playing the Tin Man and the Scarecrow, and Ms. Andrews all looked up, startled by her entrance. The rest of the cast was sprawled across the seats in the audience, whispering to each other or working on homework or watching the action on the stage, and they all looked at Natalia, too. Self-consciously, Natalia straightened her T-shirt, aware that she was red-faced and sweaty.

"You're a little late, Natalia," Ms. Andrews said.

"Sorry," Natalia said, her cheeks getting hot. "I had to finish something first, and it took longer than I thought it would." Zoe was looking away, and Natalia felt a hot flare of irritation—Zoe hadn't helped because she didn't want to be late, and now *Natalia* was late. Of course, Zoe's part was an *important* one. Not like an apple tree.

"Next time, please come in more quietly," Ms. Andrews said mildly.

"I'm sorry," Natalia said. Lately, she'd just been doing everything wrong. *Maybe I don't even deserve to be an apple tree*, she thought.

Ms. Andrews nodded in acknowledgment. "Take a seat until we get to your scene, Natalia."

Seeing Caitlin halfway down a row, Natalia picked her way past other kids and sat down next to her.

"That was so embarrassing," Natalia breathed.

"Seriously." Caitlin was reading and eating chips. She held the bag out to Natalia. "Where were you?"

Natalia took a chip and popped it into her mouth, crunching it between her teeth. It was salty and delicious; she hadn't even had time for a snack. "I had to walk the dogs," she said.

"Bleh." Caitlin made a face. "Aren't you tired of taking care of other people's dogs?"

"No, I'm not," Natalia said, realizing it was true. She was tired of *being* tired, and she thought she might have taken on more dogs than she could handle, but she still *liked* doing it. She tried to explain. "They're so sweet and funny, and each one has a personality that's totally their own. Like, Jasper wants to take care of everybody—he's always checking on Daisy, and if you stop when you're walking him, he'll come over and look up at you like he's asking if you're all right. And Daisy is just totally obsessed with squirrels. And Ruby *loves* people, so, so much, but she *hates* other dogs. And Bandit just wants everyone to take it easy and let him nap. If you sit down, he'll put his paws on your lap and try to cuddle with you, even though he's way too big."

Caitlin gave her a little smile and ate another chip. "They sound cute," she admitted. "But it still sounds like a lot of work."

"Well, yeah," Natalia said. "I love the dogs and I'll miss them, but I won't be totally sorry when their owners leave Seaview House and I get a break."

"Me neither," Caitlin said, handing Natalia the last

chip and crumpling up the empty bag. "I never get to see you lately. When the dogs leave, you should join me and Emma's study group."

"Your and *Emma's* study group?" Natalia said in surprise. Caitlin didn't dislike Emma the way she used to, but their hanging out together was new.

Caitlin shrugged. "I've learned some excellent study tricks from Emma."

"Huh," Natalia said. *It would be* great *if Caitlin and Emma ended up being really good friends,* she thought.

Up on the stage, Zoe and the others began to sing. "We're off to see the wizard, the wonderful Wizard of Oz." Zoe's voice rang out clear and strong, and Natalia felt a sort of reluctant pride. She was still kind of mad that Zoe had skipped dog walking and made Natalia late, but the extra singing practice had paid off. Her sister sounded *good* up there. Ms. Andrews stopped them and demonstrated a skipping dance step. Zoe swung right into the dance, her arms firmly linked with the kids playing the Scarecrow and the Tin Man, and Natalia felt even prouder and, weirdly, more irritated, too. Zoe had always been good at stuff. There were so many things she was better at than Natalia.

But Zoe had been kind of standoffish with other kids, an observer instead of a doer. Natalia had been the one who performed, who might be up onstage dancing around, or hanging out with other kids, practicing. Did Zoe have to be good at that, too?

It was ages later that Natalia finally got called up to the stage. She'd lost interest in seeing Zoe do the same thing over and over, and she'd gotten Caitlin and a bunch of other girls to fold fortune-tellers instead. The last one Natalia had made told Caitlin she was going to grow up to be a private detective and live in a mansion. Natalia's had said she was going to grow up to be a car salesman and live in a shack.

Even fortune-tellers had lost their appeal after a while, though, and Natalia had let her head fall against the padded red-velvet back of the theater seat and closed her eyes, tiredness washing over her. It had been an awfully long day, with a lot of walking and running in it.

She was almost asleep when Ms. Andrews called out, "Can I get the apple trees up here, please?"

She didn't know the other two apple trees. One was a boy and one a girl and they looked like they were maybe fifth graders, a little younger than Natalia. She grinned at them as they climbed onto the stage beside her. "Hey, fellow trees!"

Onstage, Ms. Andrews was all business. She pointed out where they should stand—by the time the performance came, they would be surrounded by fake trees, but for now it was just the three of them—and handed them yellow foam balls about the size of tennis balls. "We'll paint these to look like apples before the performance," she told them.

Zoe and the other main characters were still standing in the center of the stage, and Natalia tossed a ball into Zoe's face as she walked by, glancing around to make sure Ms. Andrews hadn't seen. Zoe grimaced at her and threw it back.

"If you're quite finished, girls," Ms. Andrews said, and Natalia winced. *Oops.*

Natalia had almost no lines. The scene was mostly Dorothy and the Scarecrow (it was before they'd found the others) and the First Apple Tree. The girl playing the First Apple Tree had been one who'd auditioned for Dorothy: She'd been okay, Natalia remembered, except that her singing voice wasn't very good. She already had all her lines memorized and listened intently to everything Ms. Andrews said, nodding at all the stage directions she was given. *She* would clearly only throw apples when it was called for in the script.

Natalia's main line was to say, "The nerve!" when the First Apple Tree complained about Dorothy and the Scarecrow trying to pick their apples. Then, when they finally threw their apples, she was supposed to shout, "How dare you!"

It was fun the first time. Natalia and the others stretched their arms out wide, and Zoe and the boy playing the Scarecrow mimed trying to pick apples off their "branches." There was some back-and-forth between Zoe and the First Apple Tree, and then the First Apple Tree turned to Natalia and said, sounding outraged, "Hungry! Well, how would you like to have someone come along and pick something off of you?"

Natalia drew herself up as tall as she could and looked haughtily down her nose at Zoe. *"The nerve!"* she said, even more icily than Ms. Andrews had sounded when she asked if she and Zoe were finished fooling around. Zoe's lips twitched into a smile, and Natalia felt like a silent giggle had passed between them. Something in her relaxed. She didn't *want* to be mad at Zoe.

There was some more back-and-forth, a tussle between the Third Apple Tree and the Scarecrow, and all the trees grabbing at Zoe and the Scarecrow to try to keep them from getting away. Then they finally got to throw their apples. Natalia lobbed her best dodge-ball throw at her sister. To her delight, she managed to bounce one right off Zoe's forehead. Then the Scarecrow and Zoe gathered up the "apples" and pretended to bite into them.

They ran through the scene a couple times. The first time, the Third Apple Tree dropped all his apples. The second time, the Scarecrow messed up a couple of his lines.

The stage lights were on, and the warmth made Natalia sleepy. It had been a long, long day.

She imagined the final performance. Their costumes were going to be pretty cool—the biggest costumes in the show, she'd bet, with long outstretched branches and red-painted apples. She'd wave her branches threateningly, so threateningly that maybe the audience would be just the tiniest bit scared for Dorothy . . .

"Natalia! *The nerve!*" she heard Ms. Andrews whisper sharply, and she snapped back to reality. She'd missed her cue.

"The nerve!" she said, blushing. Her voice came out more apologetic than haughty that time, but the scene moved on. Natalia still felt hot and uncomfortable, clutching her foam balls. *Ms. Andrews definitely still thinks I'm irresponsible,* she realized miserably.

She pitched the balls halfheartedly this time, and not one hit Zoe.

After the show, she and Zoe waited outside for their dad to come pick them up. It was dark out, and a chilly breeze lifted their hair and made them huddle into their jackets.

"Are you okay?" Zoe asked. "You seemed really out of it during rehearsal."

"I'm fine," Natalia told her. "Just tired."

"Me, too," Zoe said. "It was a long rehearsal. I didn't realize how much dancing I was going to have to do." There was silence for a moment, Zoe shifting back and forth as if she had something else to say. Finally, she blurted, "I'm sorry I ditched you and didn't help with dog walking. I didn't know you were going to be late."

"It's not a big deal," Natalia said. She thought about Zoe saying that she'd promised they'd take care of the dogs without checking with her and Emma, and about how she seemed to think Natalia always needed their help, and she tilted her chin defiantly. "Everything's totally fine," she said.

Chapter Eleven

On Friday, Natalia flipped through her math folder, looking for the previous day's homework. She reached the back of the folder without finding it, and her heart gave a funny, cold-feeling skip. *It wasn't there.*

She went through the pages again, more carefully. She'd done the homework, she really had. She'd even looked up examples of how to do the problems on the computer. They hadn't all made sense to her, but she thought she had probably gotten closer to getting the problems right than she had on most of her recent math assignments. But now she didn't have the worksheet at all.

Natalia thought hard. She remembered sitting at her desk, finishing her homework. Zoe had been at her desk on the other side of their bedroom, but they hadn't talked back and forth like they usually did. She wasn't *mad* at Zoe, not exactly, but she hadn't wanted to talk to her, either.

She hadn't asked Zoe for help.

Natalia had thought about it. There was one question she just couldn't get. She'd tried to figure it out by looking up videos about how to do similar problems, but they didn't help. And she knew Zoe understood the math homework.

But then she remembered Zoe saying, *That's a laugh!* her face all screwed up with anger, and she couldn't do it.

But, whether she had gotten that one problem right or not, she had finished the homework.

She had forgotten to put it in her folder. Cold certainty filled her—she could picture the paper, sitting abandoned right in the center of her desk at home—just as Ms. Patel stopped at her desk and held out her hand for Natalia's homework.

"I'm sorry," Natalia said softly. "I left my worksheet at home. I did do it."

Ms. Patel gave her a disappointed look. "Natalia, please stay and see me after class," she said.

Natalia exchanged a wide-eyed look with Caitlin, her heart sinking.

For the rest of class, she tried to pay total attention to Ms. Patel. Maybe the teacher wouldn't be mad at her if Natalia was a perfect student for the rest of the period. But she couldn't concentrate. How much trouble was she in?

When the bell rang, Natalia reluctantly walked up to Ms. Patel's desk as everyone else left for social studies.

Ms. Patel pointed at the chair next to her desk, waited for Natalia to sit down, and then sat down in the chair behind the desk. Clasping her hands on the desk in front of her, she gave Natalia a long, steady stare.

"I really did do it," Natalia said nervously.

Ms. Patel sighed. "I'm glad to hear that, Natalia, but this is part of a pattern I'm seeing with you this semester. You've been skipping assignments, and when you do them, you don't seem to understand them. You seem distracted in class. Is something going on?"

Natalia felt herself turning beet-red. "I'm trying," she said, almost whispering. She could feel her pulse pounding in her throat. "Nothing's going on. I just need to study a little more and I'll get it."

"Natalia, you need help if you're going to pass the midterms that are coming up," Ms. Patel said patiently. "I'm going to get in touch with your parents about setting up some time for tutoring."

Natalia sat bolt upright. "Please don't tell my parents," she said. "I can catch up by myself."

Ms. Patel smiled. "This isn't a punishment, Natalia," she said. "There's nothing wrong with getting help."

"Sure," Natalia muttered, slumping down in the chair. She knew her parents weren't going to think there was anything wrong with getting help, either. But Natalia didn't want to *need* help.

The meeting with Ms. Patel hadn't taken long, and Natalia just had to hurry a little on her way to class. As usual, the halls were full of the babble of voices and the squeak of sneakers on the tile floors. Lockers banged and shrieks of laughter echoed up and down the hall.

Zoe was waiting outside the social studies room, and came over. "Hey," she said. "What did Ms. Patel want to talk to you about?"

Natalia glanced at her. Zoe's face was friendly and open; it wasn't like she had any mean motive for asking about this. But Zoe had been doing great lately: being Dorothy, having an easy time at school. *Me? Not so much.*

She kept her voice as casual and happy as Zoe's was. "Ms. Patel? Nothing much. She just wanted to know when the *Wizard of Oz* performance is."

Natalia was lying, but she didn't care. The last thing she wanted was for her sister to know she was in trouble.

❧

"Come on, Jasper! Come on!" That afternoon, Emma ran down past the side of the house, racing toward the bay. Jasper ran at her heels, barking ecstatically.

"We'll catch them, Daisy!" Natalia shouted. Daisy's short legs were moving so fast they were almost a blur. Natalia felt like she was pumping her own legs just as fast, but neither of them was a match for Emma and Jasper. Far behind, Zoe and Bandit sauntered along, displaying no intention of trying to catch up. A volley of barks from the house let them know Ruby, annoyed at being left alone, had seen them.

The run was just what Natalia needed. The wind blowing off the bay into her face as she ran seemed to blow away her worries from the afternoon. Maybe Ms. Patel would call and maybe she wouldn't, but there was nothing Natalia could do about it now.

She and Daisy finally caught up with Emma and Jasper down on the beach below Seaview House. Emma was sitting near the water, building a sand castle, while Jasper was sniffing at seaweed washed up by the water's edge.

"You are ridiculously fast," Natalia said, flopping down on the sand next to Emma and trying to catch her breath. "Must be all those sports you do."

"Mmm," Emma hummed in agreement as she scooped an opening in the front of her castle. "The suicide drills they make us do in soccer, mostly. You know, where we're running back and forth, farther and farther each time."

"Ugh," Natalia said. "I'd rather be slow." She began to dig a moat around Emma's castle. The sand was cold and grainy between her fingers, but it was easy to dig.

After a little while, Zoe strolled up, Bandit tagging along behind her. She squatted down beside them, careful not to let her clothes touch the sand. "Cool castle," she said, cocking her head to one side to get a good look at it. After a moment, she took a handful of dry white sand and dribbled it over the top. "There," she said, satisfied. "That makes a nice contrast."

Bandit sat down next to Natalia, then collapsed onto her, his head in her lap. "Hey, boy," she said, twining her fingers through his thick, curly fur. His eyebrows shifted as he gazed up at her, making him look thoughtful. Affection rose up inside Natalia, and she bent down to kiss Bandit on the head. "You're such a good dog," she told him. "I'm going to miss you. I'll miss your naughty sister, too."

"I can't believe the wedding's tomorrow," Emma said. "They put it together so fast. It's at four, right?"

"Yeah, but Mom told me they want us there first thing in the morning," Natalia said. "Apparently, Rachel and her mom and Mike's mom and all the other women in the wedding have to spend the whole day getting, like, their nails and hair done, and Mike and the other guys have to spend the whole day picking up people at the airport. And with the house so full, they want somebody keeping the dogs out of trouble."

Weddings actually sound pretty fun, Natalia thought. She'd never really been into hair and nails, but it might be cool to spend a whole day being fussed over.

Zoe and Emma were both staring at her.

"What?" said Natalia, kissing Bandit on the head again. "Haven't you ever seen a girl and a dog in love before?"

"Nat, when were you going to tell us you'd promised we'd be here all day tomorrow?" Zoe said sharply.

"Um." Natalia twisted her fingers gently in Bandit's fur. She had forgotten—she'd meant to talk to them the day of the first rehearsal—but she hadn't thought it would be a problem. Zoe and Emma liked playing with the dogs as much as she did.

"Honestly!" Zoe stood up. "You can't just make plans for all three of us without checking with us first. You keep *doing* this!"

"Sorry," Natalia said. She bent forward over Bandit again, so that her hair was half covering her face.

Zoe sighed. "I promised I would help make props for *The Wizard of Oz* tomorrow morning. It'll be fun to *make* something again, after all this acting. And I don't want Ms. Andrews thinking I'm irresponsible."

"Irresponsible like me, you mean?" Natalia snapped.

Zoe glared at her. "I didn't say that," she said. "But maybe I should have. You keep making promises for us and expecting us to keep them. Maybe you should just promise things *you* can do."

"Fine." Natalia crossed her arms over her chest. "I don't need your help, anyway. I can take care of the dogs in the morning by myself."

"I was supposed to do study group with Caitlin and all those people," Emma said, her forehead creased with worry. "We'll be done way before the wedding. But I guess I could skip it if you need help in the morning."

Natalia shook her head, pushing her hair out of her face. "Don't worry about it," she told Emma, not looking at her sister. "You're right, it's my responsibility."

Emma looked dubious. "Are you sure?"

"Totally sure," Natalia told her. She took one of Bandit's ears in each hand and made them wiggle, smiling at Emma as if she were completely confident. "How much trouble could two sweet little dogs be?"

Chapter Twelve

Okay, I think I'm ready. Natalia patted the tote bag she carried as she turned the corner toward Seaview House. The whole B and B was going to be in an uproar that day, and she had brought everything she could think of to keep the dogs happy and busy: chew toys, treats, a dog brush, and a ball.

When she got to the front door of Seaview House, two women and a man, their arms full of white flowers, were ahead of her.

"Get the door for us, will you, sweetie?" one of the women asked. She and the man were holding a huge arrangement of white flowers between them. Sprays of lilies, huge puffy hydrangeas, and other flowers Natalia couldn't identify stuck out so widely that it was clearly going to barely fit through the door. The other woman held a box full of bouquets, the largest just of white roses, the others white mixed with pink and yellow. The flowers smelled heavenly.

"They're so pretty!" Natalia said enthusiastically as she held the door for them.

Inside, breakfast was still going on. Since the wedding party and most of the guests had arrived the night before, the dining room was more crowded than it had ever been previously. A waft of delightful food smells hit Natalia as soon as she walked in. There was a clatter of silverware and glasses and the noises of happy people talking. Natalia's mom and Aunt Amy were hurrying back and forth from the kitchen to the dining room, carrying platters and bowls of food. Grandma Stephenson, Natalia knew, would be in the kitchen with Uncle Brian, chopping and stirring.

Natalia's mom saw her in the doorway and came over, putting a platter of cinnamon buns down on the side table on her way.

"Hi, honey," she said. "You all set for today? Where are the others?"

"Sure," Natalia said, patting her tote bag. "I've got my trusty dog-watching supplies in here. Emma will be back soon and Zoe's outside." *It's not really a lie because "soon" could just mean before the wedding, and Zoe is outside of Seaview House . . . Oh, forget it, it is a lie,* Natalia thought, with a pang of guilt. She didn't want her mom to know she hadn't asked Zoe and Emma before she said they'd be here all day, and she didn't want them to get in trouble for not helping, either. She could just imagine how *irresponsible* Zoe would think she was then. *A lie that protects someone else is okay, isn't it? Even if you're protecting yourself, too?*

"Okay," her mom said. There was a clatter as someone dropped a fork, and she glanced toward the tables, distracted. "Ruby and Bandit are out on the screened porch. The other dogs are in their owners' rooms, but please take them outside and give them a good walk now and again before the wedding. Their owners should be back around dinnertime and will take over then." She started to go into the kitchen and then turned back to Natalia again, remembering something. "Oh, and

Rachel wanted to talk to you as soon as possible. She's in the dining room."

Rachel was sitting at one of the larger blue-painted tables with what looked like her family and her bridesmaids—the mom Natalia had seen before, a big man with gray hair who must be her dad, a teenage girl who looked like a younger version of Rachel, and two other women about Rachel's age.

"Hi, Rachel," Natalia said, walking up to them. "Are you excited?"

Rachel didn't look like she was getting married in a few hours. She was in ratty jeans and a buttoned shirt. Her hair was pulled back into a frizzy ponytail on the top of her head. But, when she looked up at Natalia, she looked incredibly happy.

"Hi, Natalia," she said. "You guys, this is Natalia. She's taking care of Ruby and Bandit for us. Natalia, this is my family and my friends Bridget and Alicia." Natalia said hello and everybody said hi back, although Natalia heard Rachel's mother say something disparaging about *those dogs!*

"I have something important to ask you." Rachel still looked happy, but her gaze was serious. "Two things, actually."

"Okay," Natalia said.

"Number one, I had Ruby and Bandit professionally groomed first thing this morning, so please, please make sure they stay clean and pretty until the wedding? When you take them out, keep them on their leashes and don't let them go down on the beach and get all sandy, okay?"

"Sure," Natalia said. That was easy enough.

"Number two," Rachel paused and grimaced. "This is actually a big thing to ask, and it's okay to say no. But I hope you'll say yes. The dogs didn't do great as ring bearers at the wedding rehearsal last night."

"Oh, that's too bad," Natalia said. She wasn't surprised, though. She couldn't picture Ruby just walking calmly down the aisle and holding still to have a ring taken off her collar.

"We thought Mike's niece, Alice, who's our flower girl, could lead them in, but she's only four and they're too big for her," Rachel explained. "You're so great with Ruby and Bandit, we hoped you could help out by leading them."

"Me?" Natalia said, stunned.

"It's a really casual wedding," Rachel assured her. "Small. You could just put on any dress, like something you might wear to school, and lead them down the aisle behind Alice. And then take them back out after we get the rings off their collars." Looking at Natalia's surprised face, she hesitated. "It's okay if you don't want to, but you'd really be helping us out. I know this is very last-minute."

"No, I want to," Natalia said firmly. She could borrow a dress from Emma so she wouldn't have to go home. She could picture herself, dressed in one of Emma's nicest dresses (Emma, unlike Natalia, took wonderful care of her clothes), leading Ruby and Bandit down the aisle, everyone's eyes on her. Rachel sighed with relief, and Natalia smiled at her. "It sounds like fun."

Ruby and Bandit were waiting for her on the screened back porch. They were both beautifully clean, with freshly done poodle cuts, their curly fur fluffy. There was a big golden bow tied around each of their necks. Bandit had climbed up onto the porch swing and fallen asleep, but Ruby was pacing across the porch. When she saw Natalia, she barked excitedly, her tail whipping back and forth, and jumped up against the screen door.

"Hey there, cutie," Natalia said, laughing as she tried to push the door open. "You've got to back up enough to let me in."

She finally wriggled her way in as Ruby shoved against her legs, licking at her hands. "Good girl," Natalia said. "Don't you look pretty?"

Ruby was wriggling with so much excitement that Natalia could hardly clip on her leash. As she scratched on the screen door, Natalia coaxed Bandit to his feet and put his leash on as well. Outside, Ruby strained toward the beach, but Natalia held her back. "Sorry, baby," she said. "We've got to stay on the sidewalk today." She led the dogs up the side lawn and to the front of Seaview House.

They walked a long circuit around the neighborhood, but Ruby kept pulling at the leash. She wanted to run, to play catch, to roll in the dirt. "I know you want to play, sweetie," Natalia said, petting her. "This is just for today, I promise. When we get back to the house, I've got some toys for you."

It took a long time to get back to Seaview House, though, with Ruby tugging Natalia toward the beach and Bandit sauntering at his usual slow pace. "I'd better run up and take Jasper and Daisy out," Natalia told the dogs once they reached the screened porch again. She opened the door and prodded them in. "I'll be right back."

Ruby, seeming outraged at the idea of going back onto the porch without being able to get off her leash, tried to wiggle through the doorway. Natalia gently pushed her back and closed the door, but Ruby pressed her face against it and whined.

"I'll be right back," Natalia promised, feeling guilty.

Almost the whole time that she was walking Jasper and Daisy, Natalia could hear Ruby barking: sad, lonely barks that sounded like they were saying, *What about me? Don't forget about me!* It was hard to enjoy Jasper and Daisy's playfulness when Ruby was so clearly miserable.

At last, though, Ruby stopped barking. *Maybe she's napping with Bandit,* Natalia thought hopefully.

She gave Jasper and Daisy a good long walk, though—that was her *responsibility,* and responsibility was going to be Natalia's new defining quality, she'd decided, no matter what Zoe thought of her—before taking them back to Seaview House. Once she had them safely in their rooms, she walked back toward the screened porch, planning ways to entertain the dogs. They could play catch with a tennis ball on the porch, she thought. There wasn't much that was breakable. And Ruby would probably enjoy a good tug-of-war with the rope dog toy Natalia had in her bag.

As soon as she rounded the corner of the house, Natalia's breath caught in her throat. For a moment, she didn't understand what she was seeing. There was a *hole* in the screened side of the porch. A big hole, as if something had burst through it. As if something had escaped. As if a *dog* had escaped.

Her heart pounding with terror, Natalia ran across the lawn. "Ruby! Bandit!" she called.

There was no answering bark. She yanked the screen door open and looked around. Bandit was back up on the porch swing, curled into a big pile of fluff. He seemed to be asleep again.

Ruby was nowhere to be seen.

"Ruby!" Natalia shouted again, slamming back out through the screen door. She looked left and right. Ruby wasn't playing on the lawn or rolling in the rich brown soil of the garden. Ruby was *gone*.

Natalia started toward the beach, then hesitated and looked back at Bandit. If he woke up, he could easily get out the hole that Ruby had made in the screen. It seemed unlikely, since so far Bandit didn't seem inclined to go *anywhere* without a lot of encouragement, but what if he did? She couldn't lose both dogs.

Could she tie him to something? Natalia went back onto the porch and looked around. There was nothing on the walls that a leash could be secured to, and all the furniture seemed like it would be too light and easily moved. She couldn't leave him alone, but she had to find Ruby. She looked wildly around. What if Ruby was hurt? The longer she was missing, the more likely something awful could happen to her. Natalia sniffed back tears, wiping her eyes with the back of her hand. What if Ruby ran out into the street?

Natalia was going to have to ask for help. She wrestled with herself for a minute. Zoe had been so perfect lately—perfect grades, perfect role in the play—and Natalia hadn't. Zoe thought she was irresponsible. She thought Natalia should keep the promises she had made herself. Natalia didn't want to have to confess to her twin that she had messed up *again*.

But despite everything, it was easy to know who would help her.

Pulling out her cell phone, she called Zoe. "I lost Ruby," she said when her sister picked up. Her voice cracked miserably.

There was a tiny pause, and then Zoe said, reassuringly, "I'm on my way. Did you call Emma yet?"

"I'm about to."

"Great. Just hang on. We'll find her."

Emma was still at her study group, but she promised she would leave right away. When she showed up a few minutes later, she had Caitlin with her. "We were

153

studying together when you called," she explained, "and Caitlin wanted to help."

"What's the dog's name?" Caitlin asked.

"Ruby," Natalia and Emma answered as Zoe arrived, breathless.

"Ruby!" Caitlin called. "Ruby!"

"I've been calling her," Natalia said miserably. "Either she can't hear or she doesn't want to come." She felt dizzy and sick with panic.

Caitlin patted her on the back. "Deep breaths, Natalia. Obviously, we need a plan." Natalia breathed deeply, in through her nose and out through her mouth, and felt her stomach settle a little.

Zoe looked thoughtful. "Okay, where would Ruby be likely to go? Natalia, you know her best. What do you think?"

"She likes the beach," Natalia said, still taking deep, slow breaths.

"She liked that little park a couple blocks away, too," Emma contributed.

"And we walked her and Bandit over to our house the other day, and Mateo gave her one of Riley's dog biscuits," Zoe remembered. "Any dog might want to go back where there's food."

"How about if Natalia checks the beach, I go to the park, and Zoe goes by your house?" Emma suggested. "Caitlin, maybe you can stay here in case she comes back, and also make sure Bandit doesn't get out?"

"Sure," Caitlin said. She was still giving Natalia a worried look, but Natalia was feeling better now that they were all in action together.

"Okay. We'll keep in touch. As soon as anyone finds anything—or finds out for sure Ruby isn't there—that person texts everyone else," Zoe said.

On the way to the beach, Natalia's heart lightened. She was sure she was going to find Ruby there. The beach was Ruby's favorite place, after all. She loved going there on walks: catching balls, trying to bite the waves, rolling in the sand. Natalia knew Ruby would go to the beach.

So it was a shock to come over the hill above the beach, a leash dangling from her hand, and to not see Ruby waiting for her.

Natalia ran down toward the water and looked

frantically in both directions. There was a cool breeze coming off the bay, and there were only a few people on the beach. An older couple was walking along the shore, picking up shells, while some younger kids chased each other across the sand.

Her phone buzzed with a text. *Ruby's not at our house,* Zoe wrote. *I asked Dad and Abuelita and the boys and none of them have seen her.*

Natalia's stomach dropped a little with disappointment, but she had thought it was a long shot that Ruby might go to their house.

She peered down the beach in both directions. Far down the shore, there was something white. It could be a dog, down by the water. Could it be Ruby? She headed in that direction, walking fast.

Her phone buzzed again. Emma. *Ruby isn't anywhere in the park.*

Natalia sighed and looked down the beach again. The white thing was definitely a dog, she could see that now. *Please let it be Ruby,* she thought. She broke into a jog.

It *was* Ruby! The big poodle was digging energetically, her white paws churning up sand. Lots and lots of dark-brown, wet sand. She was probably chasing a sand crab as it burrowed deeper and deeper into the beach.

"Ruby!" Natalia called. Ruby stopped digging and came over cheerfully, licking Natalia's hands and then standing on her hind legs with her front paws against Natalia to try to lick her face. "Yuck, no!" Natalia said, catching Ruby's sand-caked paws. She lowered them back down to the beach, then pulled out her phone. *I found her. And she's FILTHY.*

When she and Ruby got back to Seaview House, Caitlin was holding the hose. "It's too bad we can't use a bathtub," she said, "but I don't think you want to take her through the bed-and-breakfast like that."

"Especially not when everyone's getting ready for a wedding," Natalia agreed. She remembered that Rachel had asked her specifically not to let Ruby get dirty, and not to let her play in the sand, and winced guiltily. "She just went to the groomer."

Emma and Zoe were already back, too. "I can get shampoo and a hair dryer from my room," Emma suggested. She and her parents had renovated part of the attic into an apartment so that they could live a little bit away from the guests.

"Get hand soap, too," Zoe said, looking at the drooping formerly gold ribbon around Ruby's neck. "Or delicates detergent if you have it. And check the laundry room for spray starch. I might be able to salvage this ribbon."

Ruby loved her shower. Caitlin was manning the hose, and Ruby kept sticking her face right into the water, lapping it up. She even stood still while Natalia and Emma worked the shampoo deep into her fur, scrubbing to get out every bit of sand. Meanwhile, Zoe was painstakingly soaping the ribbon, tiny section by tiny section.

"Girls?" Natalia and Zoe's mom opened the door between the porch and the rest of the house and was staring at them, confused. "What are you doing to that dog?" Her eyes widened and she started to look a little panicky. "Didn't Rachel *just* have her groomed for the wedding?"

"Yes. Um." Natalia looked at Zoe and Zoe shrugged. *Better tell the truth.* "Ruby got out while I was walking Daisy and Jasper, and she got all dirty."

"While you were walking Daisy and Jasper?" Her mom was still looking confused, one eyebrow raised. "Wasn't anyone watching the other dogs? Where were Zoe and Emma?"

Zoe and Emma looked at each other. "We weren't here," Emma said softly. "Natalia was taking care of the dogs alone."

Zoe looked guilty. "She's been doing most of the dog stuff alone. We've both been really busy. I'm sorry."

Caitlin raised her hand. "I didn't have anything to do with any of that," she said. "I just came over to help today when I heard Ruby was lost."

But Natalia's mom didn't pay any attention to Caitlin. Instead, she was looking at Natalia. "But you told me the others were here today," she said.

Natalia felt herself turning bright red. "I'm sorry," she said, ashamed. "I didn't want you to worry and I thought I could handle it all by myself."

Natalia's mom's eyes were bright with anger. "I don't like this lying, Natalia," she said. "And I just got an email from your math teacher. She told me you're really struggling in math and that she wants you to come to after-school tutoring. She says you haven't been doing homework assignments." She shook her head, letting out a long breath of frustration. "I don't understand why you didn't come to your father and me earlier if you were having trouble in school."

"I . . . I just thought . . ." Natalia could hear her own voice getting softer and softer. "I wanted to handle it by myself . . ."

Natalia's mom looked at her watch. "I need to start setting up the folding chairs for the ceremony. But we're going to have a long talk about this later tonight, Natalia. I'm very disappointed in you for lying and for not doing your homework."

She hurried back into the house, and Natalia winced. "That wasn't good, you guys," she told the others.

And now she had a "long talk" with her mom and probably her dad to look forward to.

Gulp.

Chapter Thirteen

Outside the living room where the wedding ceremony was about to take place, Natalia held on to Ruby and Bandit's special golden leashes. After her bath with the hose, Ruby was looking just as clean and groomed as Bandit, and Zoe, using a special art-girl magic, had even made her bedraggled ribbon look fresh and crisp again.

Switching the leashes to hold them both in one hand, Natalia smoothed down her skirt with the other hand as she waited for the processional music to begin. Emma had lent her a sparkly blue dress that she had worn to some kind of sports award banquet last spring, and Zoe had fixed her hair. Natalia felt warmly conscious that she was looking unusually pretty and well dressed. *Perfect for a wedding.*

She hadn't forgotten that she was in trouble with her

parents, she thought, taking a leash in each hand again. And at school, and probably in the theater program, too. But it was going to be a beautiful wedding, and Natalia figured she might as well enjoy herself while she could.

Alice, the four-year-old flower girl, was standing directly in front of her, her blonde head crowned with flowers. Suddenly, she turned around and frowned forbiddingly at Natalia. "Is that bad dog going to jump up on me?" she said accusingly. "She jumped up on me yesterday."

Natalia shook her head solemnly. "I've got a good hold on her," she said. Somehow, she knew which dog Alice was accusing.

"She put her big feet right on me," Alice told her. "I almost fell down. She's a very bad dog." She glared at Ruby, who panted happily and wagged her tail.

"She just got excited," Natalia explained. "She's not a bad dog." She rumpled Ruby's ears and added, "Not *very* bad, anyway."

Alice looked dubious. "You'll make sure she doesn't jump on me? I don't want to fall down during the wedding."

Natalia nodded. "I promise," she said. "I will be responsible for her."

Alice gave her a searching look and then nodded. "Okay. Thank you," she said, and turned back around as the music changed.

Now that Alice wasn't looking at her, Natalia let herself grin at how serious the little girl had been. Alice was *so* cute.

The doors to the living room opened. Natalia almost gasped. The room seemed transformed, bright with hanging gold fabric and fragrant with gorgeous white flowers. The audience turned, then rose to their feet, waiting.

Aunt Amy was just inside the doors. She waved Alice on, and the little girl walked in with slow, measured steps, taking one handful of rose petals at a time from the basket she carried and scattering them on the floor.

Ruby tried to charge after her, but Natalia held her back. Maintaining a tight hold on Ruby's leash and gently tugging Bandit forward, she followed Alice down the aisle, keeping time with the little girl's steps.

When they got to the front of the room, the minister

was standing at the very end of the aisle. To his left were Mike and his groomsmen. Alice turned to the other side and Natalia grabbed the dogs' leashes right by their collars to keep them close and followed the little girl.

The bridesmaids came next, lining up beside Natalia and Alice. Finally, when everyone else was in place, the music changed again, and Rachel, her arm twined through her father's, came slowly down the aisle. She was wearing a lacy white dress, and, when her eyes met Mark's, they both looked really, really happy. Natalia suddenly felt tears spring to her eyes. She felt sentimental and thrilled, and she hoped they would be so happy forever.

Seeing Rachel, Ruby gave a bark and tried to charge forward. A friendly laugh spread through the audience. Natalia gripped Ruby's leash tightly. "No, Ruby," she whispered. "Sit." Miraculously, Ruby did.

Finally, the dogs' (and Natalia's) big moment came. "Do you have the rings?" the minister asked. Mike gestured to Natalia to come closer, and she led the dogs toward him. Ruby jumped up, putting her paws on his chest, and the audience laughed softly again, a happy, gentle sound. "Down, Ruby!" Natalia whispered, and, once again, Ruby listened.

I may be a natural dog trainer, Natalia thought. She imagined herself, years in the future, surrounded by perfectly trained dogs. They'd do tricks she taught them, and obey her every whim. People would pay her hundreds of dollars, since she'd be the only one who could make their difficult dogs cooperate.

It seemed like a pretty awesome future, Natalia thought, watching Mike take the rings from the dogs' collars and rumple their ears affectionately. But first she'd have to make it through middle school.

Gꩄ

The rest of the wedding was equally beautiful. Uncle Brian had done wonders with the food. There was dancing, and toasts with champagne, and everyone seemed incredibly happy. Natalia overheard several people saying they would come back to Seaview House, or asking her mother or Aunt Amy for business cards in case they wanted to schedule a future event. Seaview House's first wedding (first wedding as a B and B, that was, since the family had been getting married there for generations) was a huge success.

But all the excitement of the day drained straight out of Natalia that evening when she was sitting at her own family's kitchen table, her mom and dad and Abuelita sitting across from her with serious, concerned faces.

She had Zoe beside her, though, and that was a comfort. As she thought this, Zoe leaned toward her, nudging their shoulders together.

"What's going on, Natalia?" her dad asked.

"I've been having trouble in math," Natalia confessed, looking down at the table instead of at her dad. "I got so busy that I just couldn't keep up. I didn't understand the assignments and I was so tired I forgot to do them sometimes."

"It was partly my fault," Zoe said protectively. "Emma and I were supposed to help with the dog walking, and we kept putting it all on Natalia."

"No, I promised you guys would do stuff without checking with you first," Natalia said, looking up. Her problems weren't Zoe and Emma's fault. "That wasn't fair."

"You should have come to us," Natalia and Zoe's mom told them sternly. "It's our job to help you. We could have helped you organize your time and gotten you tutoring in math before things got to this point."

"I know," Natalia said, hanging her head again.

Her mom sighed. "I'm afraid you're going to have to quit *The Wizard of Oz*. I'm sorry, but Ms. Patel's after-school tutoring is at the same time as rehearsals."

"That's terrible," Zoe said, glaring at her mom. "Natalia loves theater club. And it won't be as fun without her."

Natalia felt a little sad—and embarrassed at the idea of having to quit—but she was surprised not to feel worse. She had ached inside at how badly she had blown the audition. "It's okay," she told Zoe. "I'll start fresh with the next show and I'll work really hard. Maybe I'll get a better part."

"In any case, I'll be glad when all those dogs check out," their dad said. "They took up way too much time that you needed for other things."

Her mom nodded. "I think having pets at the B and B is an experiment that failed."

"Oh no!" Natalia burst out. Everyone looked

surprised at her objection. "Didn't you hear people saying at the wedding how excited they were to find a pet-friendly inn?" she said. "If Seaview House is going to be successful, that could be a big draw."

Her mom looked touched. "I appreciate that you want to help out, Natalia," she said. "But it can't come at the expense of your schoolwork."

"I can help," Zoe said. "*Really* help, not just sort of help, like I did this time. And I bet Emma will feel the same way."

Abuelita, who had been listening quietly, spoke up. "I'd be happy to help, too," she said. Natalia's mom started to object, but Abuelita shook her head at her. "No arguments," she said. "I'm still strong, even if I am getting old. And a good walk in the afternoon will be excellent exercise."

Natalia smiled at her grandmother. "Thanks, Abuelita," she said. She looked at Zoe, too, and at her parents. "And thank you, all. Next time, I'll do better."

She felt like a huge weight had been lifted off her shoulders. All this time, Natalia had been so afraid of asking for help. She had felt like she had to be responsible, and that things would fall apart if she let anyone know there were problems.

But now everyone knew she needed help. And it was going to be fine. She would catch up in math, and she wouldn't have to tell any more lies. And next time, she would know her lines for her audition.

And maybe she would be an expert dog trainer one day, too. At the very least, it seemed likely there would be cute dogs to play with at Seaview House again soon.

Chapter Fourteen

"Oh, Auntie Em!" Zoe said, gazing around the stage. "There's no place like home!"

The audience burst into applause, and the curtain fell. Natalia was clapping so hard her hands hurt.

The Stephenson-Martinez family took up a whole row in the auditorium. Everyone was there: Emma and Natalia, Mateo and Tomás, Uncle Brian and Aunt Amy, Natalia and Zoe's mom and dad, Grandma Stephenson and Abuelita, and even Uncle Dean and Aunt Bonnie. They were all dressed up and cheering for Zoe.

The curtain went up again, and Zoe and the rest of the cast came out and bowed. Caitlin was wearing her sparkly Glinda costume and looking pleased with herself. The apple trees—they had cast another Second Apple Tree—seemed hot and sweaty from wearing their bulky tree outfits, but they were laughing. Darcy had been a really good Wicked Witch, Natalia admitted to herself. Probably just as good as Natalia could have been.

And Zoe had been terrific. Natalia's twin, who was usually on the edges of things, observing so carefully but keeping herself a little apart, had shone onstage. Looking at her sister's happy face as she bowed again and again, Natalia clapped even harder.

❧

Afterward, following celebratory ice cream cones at Sweet Jane's with the whole family, Emma, Zoe, and Natalia decided to walk home together. It was still warm enough for the night walk to be comfortable, but Natalia tucked her hands into her jacket pockets. She could feel that winter was coming.

"I almost forgot my lines in the scene where I meet the Scarecrow," Zoe was saying. "Did you notice?"

Emma shook her head. "I thought you were great."

"Are you fishing for compliments, evil twin?" Natalia asked. Under the streetlights, their shadows looked huge and dark.

Zoe made a face. "I'm pretty sure *you're* the evil twin," she said. "*Lying*. Getting bad grades. Cavorting with that naughty puppy Ruby."

Natalia shrugged. "That was weeks ago," she said. "I'm pretty much caught up in math now, and I haven't told any lies for ages."

"A model citizen," Emma agreed.

With a sudden rush of affection, Natalia wrapped her arms around her sister and her cousin. "Thank you. Really," she said. "I never could have done it without you. I need you guys. Both of you."

"Well, duh," Zoe answered. "You can't manage without us."

"Zoe!" Emma said reprovingly.

Zoe grinned. "And we need you, too, of course," she said quickly. "The Three Musketeers. Two of them evil twins."

"I miss the naughty puppy, though," Natalia said thoughtfully. "But a couple with a schnauzer booked a room at Seaview House for two weeks from now, so that'll be fun. Or maybe we could expand the business.

There's got to be a lot of people in Waverly who need dog walkers."

"I don't know . . ." Emma said, frowning.

"Aw, come on," Natalia went on. "Soccer season is ending. The play is over. How are you guys going to fill up your time now?"

"I'm not worried," Zoe said drily. "You're definitely going to get us involved in some kind of scheme before long. I can sense it."

Natalia felt full of love. Her two favorite people in the whole world, walking beside her. "Well, yeah," she said. "Probably. After all, together we can do anything."

Don't miss the next Like Sisters book!

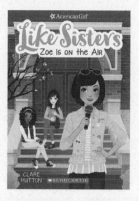

Zoe Is on the Air

Zoe and Emma are hosting an advice segment on their school's morning news show. Friendship drama? Sibling rivalry? School trouble? Zoe and Emma know just what to do! But when some of their advice starts to backfire, Zoe needs new answers—and fast!

Read Emma's story!

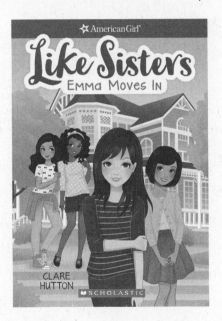

ChapteR One

Things We Absolutely HAVE To Do:

1. Have a cookout

Well, that will be easy, Emma thought, wiggling her feet under the airline seat in front of her. By the time she and her parents finally got to Waverly, Uncle Luis would be flipping burgers on the grill while her mom's twin sister, Aunt Alison, and all the cousins arranged salads and desserts on the big outdoor trestle table.

Last year, her family had gotten there the evening before the annual family barbecue, and Emma and her two favorite cousins, twins Natalia and Zoe, had made up their own brownie recipe. They mixed in not just walnuts and chocolate chips, but dried pineapple, coconut, raisins, peanuts, and marshmallows. It had been Natalia's idea—Zoe had been skeptical, and Emma had thought maybe they should play it safe and follow the real recipe—but Natalia had insisted, and she'd been right. The brownies had been delicious. Emma's mouth watered at the memory.

2. Swim

Back home in Seattle, the water was too cold to swim in the ocean. Emma swam in indoor swimming pools, competing in relays and races. It was fun, and she was good at it. She liked the smell of chlorine and the stretch of her muscles. Swimming in the warm, sun-splashed water of the Chesapeake Bay with Natalia and Zoe was even better, though.

3. Sparklers

At night after the barbecue, everyone—even the grown-ups—would light sparklers out in the front yard of Zoe and Natalia's house, writing their names in light. It was tradition, and their family cared about tradition.

4. Bonfire on the beach

Some evening this week, when the weather was just right, they would build a fire of driftwood on the beach and toast marshmallows to make s'mores. Natalia liked hers so dark they were almost black, and Zoe preferred hers untoasted, but Emma would turn hers patiently until they were a perfect, even golden brown all the way around.

5. Knitting with Grandma Stephenson

Over Christmas, Grandma had started all three of them making scarves. Emma had chosen blue and white; Zoe, black and purple; and Natalia, red and turquoise. Emma had tried to finish the scarf on her own after she and her parents had gone back home, but the yarn had gotten tangled and she'd dropped too many stitches. Finally, she'd given up in frustration. It was too hard, and not as much fun by herself.

A pang went through Emma's chest at the thought of her grandmother. Back in the spring, Grandma Stephenson had fallen on the stairs of Seaview House, her big, wonderful Victorian home, and broken her hip. She was okay—everyone said she was going to be just fine—but she had left Seaview House and moved in with Zoe and Natalia's family, where their other grandma, Uncle Luis's mom, Abuelita, already lived.

Emma's mom had told her the living situation was only temporary, but it had been going on for months now. What if Grandma wasn't really okay? No, her mom wouldn't have said Grandma was going to be fine unless it was true.

But the beautiful house where generations of Emma's family had lived was shuttered and silent. Emma's mom said that Seaview House would be too big for Grandma Stephenson to take care of by herself even when she was fully recovered.

At the thought of Seaview House empty, Emma felt her throat go tight, and she swallowed back the feeling before it turned into tears. It would be silly to cry over a *house* when the important thing was that Grandma was okay. Determined not to think about Seaview House, she turned back to her list.

Emma hesitated, her pencil resting on the paper, not sure about whether to leave knitting on the list. They could knit just as well in the living room of Natalia and Zoe's house as they had in the parlor at Seaview House, of course. But maybe Grandma didn't feel like doing projects anymore since she'd been hurt. Should she scratch that one out?

Even if Grandma hadn't changed, knitting wasn't really a summer thing, and Natalia and Zoe might have already finished their scarves with Grandma while Emma wasn't there. Emma pushed away the fleeting thought, *Not fair.* She knew she couldn't expect everyone in Waverly to just wait for her to come back before doing anything fun together.

Next to her, Emma's dad gave a little snore, and she glanced up as he slouched farther down against the airplane window, his glasses perched crookedly on his nose and his mouth open. Emma's mom looked up from her laptop screen at the same time and caught Emma's eye just as her dad snorted. They both giggled.

"He's been working hard on the new menu," her mom said. "This nap is just what he needs. He'll be ready to ride the waves with you girls by the time we get there."

Emma grinned. Her dad had the most ridiculous bathing suit—bright pink with wild purple and turquoise tropical flowers on it—but she liked how he came out into the water or onto the beach in his crazy bathing suit and played with them, instead of just hanging out with the other grown-ups. Last summer, he'd helped them and Zoe and Natalia's little brothers build a huge sand castle with a pebble-covered drawbridge and turrets reaching up to the sky.

She felt a sudden surge of affection for her parents. She liked their tight little unit of three: her mother, her father, and herself.

But sometimes she couldn't help envying Zoe and Natalia for having not just their parents and each other, but also their little brothers (even if Tomás and Mateo were bratty sometimes), and Grandma Stephenson, and Abuelita, and living near Uncle Dean and Aunt Bonnie, whose own kids were mostly away at college and brand-new jobs. They had tons of family, right in their town. Right in their *house*.

They—the whole of her mom's side of the family, except for Emma and her parents—all lived in Waverly, a small town on the Chesapeake Bay, where the family had lived for generations. Natalia and Zoe went to the school where Emma's mom and their mom (Aunt Alison) had gone, along with their brother (Uncle Dean). The school was right down the street from Seaview House, where her mom's grandparents, and more generations before that, had lived.

It must be nice to *belong* somewhere so much that everyone knew you and you knew every inch of the whole town. Emma lived in Seattle now, but two years ago they'd lived in San Francisco, before her mom got a job at a different law firm. Natalia and Zoe had lived in the same house their whole lives.

Emma's mom went back to her computer screen, squinting at a long, boring-looking work document. And Emma picked up her pencil and looked down at her list again.

6. Finish the Violet story

She and Natalia had started a story last summer—all about a girl named Violet who had a talking dog that only Violet could understand and the trouble he'd gotten her into. They had laughed a lot writing it, and Zoe had drawn really funny pictures of steam coming out of Violet's ears because she was so angry and of her innocent-faced dog looking as if he had no idea what had happened or *why* everything was such a mess.

Did Natalia still have the story? They hadn't had time to work on it over Christmas. A little ball of anxiety expanded in Emma's chest. There was never enough *time.* In just a week, she'd be on a plane heading back to Seattle again.

The pilot's voice came over the intercom, interrupting her thoughts. "We're now approaching our final descent into Baltimore. Please return your seatbacks to their upright position and secure tray tables to the seatback in front of you."

There was a ton more she'd meant to write, but she was out of time again. Quickly, Emma scribbled the most important thing.

7. Cousin pact

There were so many more things she could have listed, so many things she wanted to fit into the one week they'd have with the rest of the family. But they'd make time for the pact.

She latched the tray table and put her seat upright as her mom shut down her laptop. Next to her, her dad yawned himself awake.

"How're you doing, kiddo?" he asked. "Excited to get to the house and see everybody?"

"Yeah," said Emma. She folded her list and stuffed it into the pocket of her backpack. "I just wish we could stay longer this time." She saw her parents exchange a look and added, "I know we can't. It would be fun to be with Natalia and Zoe for longer, though."

She understood why they could only come to Waverly for a few days over Christmas and for a week in the summer. Her dad was the head chef at Harvest Moon, a restaurant specializing in comfort food in Seattle, and her mom was an environmental lawyer who worked to protect the wetlands. They didn't get much time off, and Waverly was far away from Seattle. Her parents had gone over it with her a million times when she was younger and didn't understand why she couldn't see her cousins more often.

"There's a lot of stuff I want to do when we're there," she tried to explain, "and I know I won't see Natalia and

Zoe again till Christmas. I try to cram everything in, but there's never quite enough time."

Emma's dad patted her back, and her mom reached out and tucked a strand of Emma's long hair behind her ear. "We never get quite enough time with the people we love," she said sympathetically, "but try not to worry about deadlines and fitting everything you want to do in. Just concentrate on spending time with your cousins and having fun."

Emma nodded, feeling anticipation begin to spread through her. She *would* have fun. The plane's wheels hit the runway with a bump, and she realized that the whole golden, glorious week with the family was spread out before her, about to begin.